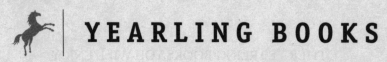

YEARLING BOOKS

Since 1966, Yearling has been the

leading name in classic and award-winning

literature for young readers.

With a wide variety of titles,

Yearling paperbacks entertain, inspire,

and encourage a love of reading.

VISIT

WWW.RANDOMHOUSE.COM/KIDS

**TO FIND THE PERFECT BOOK, PLAY GAMES,
AND MEET FAVORITE AUTHORS!**

OTHER YEARLING BOOKS YOU WILL ENJOY

CROOKED RIVER
Shelley Pearsall

TROUBLE DON'T LAST
Shelley Pearsall

DONUTHEAD
Sue Stauffacher

DOGS DON'T TELL JOKES
Louis Sachar

BELLE PRATER'S BOY
Ruth White

BARRY, BOYHOUND
Andy Spearman

HOOT
Carl Hiaasen

ALL SHOOK UP

Shelley Pearsall

A YEARLING BOOK

All rights reserved. Published in the United States by Yearling,
an imprint of Random House Children's Books, a division of Random House, Inc., New York.
Originally published in hardcover by Alfred A. Knopf,
an imprint of Random House Children's Books, in 2008.

Yearling and the jumping horse design are registered trademarks of Random House, Inc.

Visit us on the Web! www.randomhouse.com/kids

Educators and librarians, for a variety of teaching tools, visit us at www.randomhouse.com/teachers

The Library of Congress has cataloged the hardcover edition of this work as follows:
Pearsall, Shelley.
All shook up / Shelley Pearsall.
p. cm.
Summary: When thirteen-year-old Josh goes to stay with his father in Chicago for a
few months, he discovers—to his horror—that his dad has become an Elvis impersonator.
ISBN 978-0-375-83698-5 (trade) — ISBN 978-0-375-93698-2 (lib. bdg.) —
ISBN 978-0-375-84954-1 (e-book)
[1. Fathers and sons—Fiction. 2. Single-parent families—Fiction. 3. Elvis Presley impersonators—
Fiction. 4. Schools—Fiction. 5. Friendship—Fiction. 6. Chicago (Ill.)—Fiction.] I. Title.
PZ7.P3166Als 2008
[Fic]—dc22
2007022931

ISBN 978-0-440-42139-9 (pbk.)

Printed in the United States of America
10 9 8 7 6 5
First Yearling Edition

**For my dad,
an original Elvis fan**

Contents

1. Welcome to My World 1

2. Sideburns and Orange Parrots 4

3. A Big Hunk of Love for Chicago 12

4. It's Now or Never 17

5. Shaking Things Up 22

6. King of the Jungle 32

7. I Ain't Askin' Much of You 41

8. The Domino Effect 52

9. Jerry's Blue Suede Shoes 59

10. Trouble 63

11. Trouble, Continued 74

12. City Street Blues 79

13. I Forgot to Remember 82

14. Peace, Love, and Vegetarian Spaghetti 88

15. Solitaire 100

16. Winning and Losing 106

17. Hound Dog and Ivory 114

18. Viv's Vintage 122

19. Signs of the Zodiac 133

20. Watch Out for an Unexpected Surprise 140

21. Words 144

22. Sweepstakes 149

23. Return to Sender 156

24. Blue Hawaii 163

25. Ivory's Advice 169

26. Elvis Has Left the Building 178

27. Just Pretend 184

28. Cheerleaders and Cowboys 189

29. Hurt 196

30. Why Tell Elvis Everything? 200

31. Hit or Miss 206

32. Rhinestone Sneakers 212

33. Jerry Denny as the King 220

34. Such a Night 226

35. Just the Two of Us 230

36. Separate Ways 236

37. Elvisly Yours 242

38. Viva Las Vegas 250

A Little More About Elvis 259

1. Welcome to My World

Looking back, I would say everything in my life changed the summer I turned thirteen and my dad turned into Elvis.

I'd heard people say thirteen was an unlucky number, and from the very beginning, that seemed to be true. I'd been thirteen for less than twenty-four hours when the phone call came from Florida about my grandma taking a fall on the steps of the Shadyside Episcopal Church and breaking her hip. That same day, somebody swiped my bike from the rack at the city pool because—yes—I'd stupidly left it unlocked. And then my mom decided to ship me off to Chicago for four months so she could rush to Florida to take care of my grandma.

Before arriving in Illinois in August, I didn't know anything about my dad being Elvis. Well, that's not quite true. I knew there were people who pretended to be Elvis.

You know—sideburns, sunglasses, twisting hips, jiggly legs, and all. But I never thought my own dad would become one of them.

Neither did my mother, or she probably wouldn't have put me on that plane. I'd have gone to Shadyside Villas instead, where I could have stayed with her and a lot of nice old people while we waited for Grandma's hip to recover.

But my dad, in his usual style, didn't mention a word about Elvis when my mom called him. "Great. No problem. Sure. Josh can stay with me," he must have told her on the phone—while I stood on the other side of the kitchen doorway crossing my fingers behind my back, whispering, "No, say no" under my breath. As they were talking, I could hear my mom clattering a spoon around and around a mixing bowl, loudly making something for dinner. She never spoke to my father without sounding extremely busy.

"So you don't mind keeping Josh?" I heard her say. "Until Shirley's better? The doctors told me it could be a few months. He'll have to be enrolled in school. Are you sure this isn't going to be a problem?"

Keep Josh. That phrase again. Like I was somebody's pet guinea pig or prize Chihuahua getting passed back and forth. Keep Josh. Take Josh. Pick up Josh.

Note to my parents: Why not ask Josh what he would like to do?

But after eight years of being shipped between two houses almost a thousand miles apart, I knew it was pretty much useless to say anything. I was the SHARED KID and both of my parents liked me better if I seemed okay with their arrangement. So that's why I ended up telling my mom I was fine with living in Chicago for a while and staying with my dad and even going to a different school. Although I wasn't really fine with any of those things. Especially not the new school.

2. Sideburns and Orange Parrots

My dad said he would meet me near the Arrivals gate at the airport. The plane got there on time. I got there on time.

My dad didn't.

This wasn't any big surprise. Every year, I flew from Boston to Chicago to visit my father, usually during Christmas vacation and the last few weeks of August, and my dad had never once been in the right place at the right time. When I was younger, one of the flight attendants would bring me to Airport Security if my dad wasn't anywhere in sight when we landed. I was one of those crackling announcements you always hear over the airport loudspeakers. "Mr. Denny, please meet your party at Airport Security, *crackle, crackle*, Mr. Denny, please meet your . . ." That party was me.

Back then, sitting around the security office wasn't so bad because they usually gave out free cookies and juice

4

boxes to keep abandoned kids quiet and unpanicked. But I was thirteen now, and I wasn't about to be treated like a lost kid in desperate need of a tropical fruit punch.

So I didn't hang around by the gate. That was the trick, I had decided. Since I didn't need an airline babysitter anymore, I just tugged my carry-on bag over my shoulder and headed quickly for the baggage claims area, trying to look like I was somebody who traveled a lot and knew what he was doing.

This time, Dad spotted me first. I was waiting for my suitcases to come around the baggage carousel when, out of the corner of my eye, I noticed this guy with strange black hair wildly waving his arms as he hurried toward me.

Note: The last time I saw my dad's hair, it was brown. Light brown. And thinning a little on the top.

"Josh! Josh!"

Before I could say a word, I was wrapped up in one of Dad's garlic-and-cigarette-smoke hugs. My dad works with smokers and he eats out a lot, which you can tell just by getting close to him. He is also into big, manly hugs. This is the exact opposite of my mom and her family, who pat your back lightly or shake your hand when they meet you.

Note to Dad: I prefer the way my mom acts.

When my father finally stepped back and I got another look at him, I couldn't even think of what to say that would be polite. Or wouldn't hurt his feelings. He was wearing a blue Hawaiian shirt with orange parrots (parrots!) all over it, and jeans that were too tight for an adult, in my opinion, and scuffed, grass-stained white sneakers without socks. But it was his hair that I couldn't believe when I saw it close up. (Remember, I didn't know anything about him being Elvis at this point.)

I couldn't tell if he was hoping to look younger, or more in style, or if he went to a discount hair-cutting place or what, but it was completely embarrassing to see what he'd done to himself.

Picture a hairstyle that an outdated country-western singer would wear. It was an extra shiny black color. Think jet-black. Or oil slick black. Or overdid it with Hair Color for Men black. And even worse, he had grown triangle-shaped sideburns down each cheek. They reached almost to the edge of his jaw (I'm being serious). And I swear it looked like maybe there was a little black eyeliner traced under his eyes, and I didn't even want to think about that. *Jeesh.*

"Your hair's different," I said uncomfortably, trying to avoid checking out his eyes again.

"Long story," he answered, draping one arm across my shoulders. "I'll fill you in on all the details later. Let's get out of here." He started heading out of the baggage area. "My car's in a no-parking zone. Probably covered in tickets by now. I got stuck in a traffic jam on the way here, and then when I got to the airport, I opened up my wallet and realized I didn't have one single dollar to pay the parking attendant. Not one stinkin' dollar," he repeated, giving me one of his goofy grins. "Forgot to go to the bank yesterday, doesn't it figure?" My dad squeezed my shoulders again. "You're getting so daggone tall, Joshua Greenwood. Every time I see you, I swear I'm getting shorter." He says this every time I visit.

If I hadn't reminded Dad about my luggage, we would have headed to the car without it. My mom is the exact opposite. She would have picked me up on time and had plenty of change for the parking attendant, and she would probably be carrying a Post-it note that said REMEMBER JOSH'S LUGGAGE. My mom is the Post-it Note Queen. The dashboard of her car is always lined with little notes in various colors like rows of international flags: BUY BREAD & EGGS. CALL DENTIST FOR JOSH. PICK UP NEW PRESCRIPTION. CANCEL CABLE. BRING COOKIES TO BOARD MEETING.

"Luggage," I said to my dad, jerking my thumb toward the baggage conveyor.

"Right. That would help, wouldn't it?" Dad laughed at himself. Because I was staying longer on this visit, I'd brought a lot more than usual. Dad tugged my suitcases off the conveyor belt, one by one, and it took both of us to start pulling them down the corridor. Good movie title: *Josh's Life in Three Suitcases and One Carry-on Bag.*

As we passed people who were hurrying to their flights, I couldn't shake the uncomfortable feeling that everybody who walked by us was noticing my dad. I caught people checking out the parrots and the sideburns and then pretending to look away before they started cracking up.

And I could tell they were probably glancing back over their shoulders, too, craning their necks like ostriches once we'd gone by, just to get a second glimpse of the weird-looking country-western guy with the fairly normal kid walking next to him. *Why's that kid with that goofy guy?* That's what they were probably thinking.

Normally, I'm not the kind of person who spends a lot of time worrying about how I look, because there isn't a lot to pick on. My hair is nothing special, just short, a little wavy, and light brown—like my dad's hair before the bad dye job. I don't have any of the Big Three yet: Zits. Glasses. Braces. My feet are on the large side, but I'm one of those people who likes wearing my jeans long anyway. About an inch dragging on the ground under my heels, getting frayed and worn, is perfect. It's a habit that drives my mom crazy.

As more gawking people passed us, I could feel my face getting warm. Why had I worn one of my bright orange soccer sweatshirts? Why not dark blue or, better yet, gray? I reached up and flattened the hair across my forehead, hoping to cover up more of my face. I hadn't gotten a real haircut since the beginning of the summer, so this kind of worked. Keeping my eyes focused on the red and blue diamonds of the airport carpet, I imagined myself blending in, the way lizards blend into trees.

Then it happened.

Two women walked by us, and I was jerked out of red-and-blue-diamond land when I heard one of them say extra loudly to the other, "That guy looks just like Elvis. Look back at the guy in the Hawaiian shirt, Dianne. Hurry before he gets too far ahead. Look."

But here's the part I couldn't believe: My dad turned around, waved at these two strange women, and said in a smooth Southern drawl, "Hey, darlings, you talking to the King?"

The suitcase I was pulling slammed right into the back of my ankles.

Elvis.

I'm just
a hunk, a hunk
of burning love . . .
—"Burning Love," 1972

3. A Big Hunk of Love for Chicago

Trust me, right at that moment, I didn't really want an explanation for why my dad was pretending to be Elvis Presley, the King of Rock and Roll. If you have to choose between standing around with somebody who is being a complete *hunk-a hunk-a* burning shame in public or getting as far away from the situation as you can, you take the second option. Always.

I started walking again. Fast. Trying to stay a good foot or two ahead of my dad. I didn't look back, even as he kept talking to me.

"Hey, Speedy Gonzales," he hollered.

"I'm tired," I said over my shoulder.

"Well, then slow down a little."

"I just want to get to the car."

All the way there, I planned how I was going to tell Dad that, despite what he might think, I was not a

12

dumb little kid anymore and he'd better stop doing things that embarrassed me. I had a long list of examples:

Embarrassing Things My Dad Does

1. Hums loudly in public places.

2. Wears sneakers without socks in the summer (has hairy ankles).

3. Answers the phone too loudly or with some bizarre greeting other than hello, such as "Jerry's Pizza Shop," "The Shoeshine Man," or "93.5 FM, you are on *The Jerry Denny Show*"—that sort of thing.

4. Puts his arm around my shoulders as if I'm still five.

5. Introduces me to people as "Joshua Aaron Greenwood, my son from Boston," which always leads to the usual divorce conversations. Why couldn't he just say, "This is Josh"?

And I would also make sure he got the message that I didn't like his pretending-to-be-Elvis act. Or whatever he was doing to be funny this time.

When we reached the car, it had a neon orange parking ticket stuck underneath the windshield wiper. Dad whipped the ticket off the windshield. "Dammit, dammit, dammit."

Note: My dad tries his best not to swear when I'm visiting, but 99.9 percent of the time he forgets. When he forgets, his swearing is one of the things I like about him.

I tried to jam the suitcases into the backseat of his small car, which was already crowded with junk. He's driven the same dark blue Honda with the cat scratches on the trunk for as far back as I can remember.

"Just wedge your suitcases around whatever's sitting back there," my dad hollered. Right. There were two big stereo speakers, wadded-up fast-food wrappers, newspapers, a small lunch cooler, and about a dozen ceramic coffee mugs scattered across the floor of his backseat.

I think you can tell a lot about people from their coffee mugs. For instance, on the floor of Dad's Honda, there was a gold-edged mug that said TOP NOVEMBER SALESMAN, MURPHY'S SHOES. Others showed scenic places my dad had visited over the years, like Niagara Falls, St. Louis, and Myrtle Beach. One mug had the words HAPPY 40TH BIRTHDAY and another COFFEE: GROUNDS FOR DIVORCE. I shoved that one farther under the backseat junk and climbed into the front.

"All set?" Dad started the car and Elvis's voice suddenly blasted out of the speakers, almost flattening us and half of O'Hare International Airport.

A-WELL-A, BLESS MY SOUL,
WHAT'S WRONG WITH ME?

Letting out a string of swearwords, Dad reached for the knobs, trying to find the volume. The air conditioner roared on instead.

I'M ITCHING LIKE A MAN . . .

As the song boomed out of the speakers, he tried hitting several controls at once. All the people who were standing on the curb turned to stare at us, mouths open, and a ticket cop started walking slowly toward the car.

I'M IN LOVE—

Oh god. I slid down farther in my seat.

I'M ALL SHOOK UP—

Right after that, the music cut off. But I swear you could still hear "UP, UP, UP" bouncing through the terminal and ricocheting off the windows. "Sorry about that," Dad said, glancing nervously at me while the Honda lurched away from the curb, with the entire city of Chicago watching us and shaking their heads. *Freak family.*

"Just listening to a few tunes on the way here," he added, as if that explained everything, as if every dad drove around Chicago with Elvis blasting out of his stereo. "It's a long drive, you know."

I leaned back in my seat and closed my eyes, giving Dad the big hint that I really didn't want to be around him right at the moment—and since I couldn't jump out of a moving vehicle heading onto the freeway at fifty miles per hour, closing my eyes was the best I could do.

I thought about how things would have been completely different if I had gone to Florida with my mom. How, right then, we'd probably be eating at the little seafood place with those Sharks of the World paper place mats I liked to collect when I was younger. How we'd play cards at night on my grandma's patio with the moths smacking themselves silly against the screens. How there was fresh-squeezed orange juice in the morning.

Note: I know this sounds like a dumb thing to feel nostalgic about, but trust me, orange juice tastes different in Florida.

Next to me, I could hear Dad making all of his nervous sounds, tapping his fingers on the steering wheel and fiddling with the air-conditioning. "Josh," he said after it had been silent for about five seconds. "There's something important I need to tell you about. Do you want to hear it now or later?"

I clenched my eyes a little tighter, pretending to be tired. "Later."

4. It's Now or Never

Later turned out to be the McDonald's where Dad stopped for a quick cup of coffee after borrowing two bucks from me. We were sitting in a booth and I was rolling straw paper into little balls and putting them in a row like football linemen when my dad said in a completely calm voice, "I didn't exactly know how to tell your mother this news when we talked before, but, well . . . I lost my job at the beginning of May."

What?

I looked up from the table, totally shocked. Dad had worked as a salesman for Murphy's Shoes since he and my mom were together. The store's motto was "In Step with Chicago for over Thirty Years." I could still remember the sharp smell of leather and shoe polish when you opened the glass doors. Old stoop-backed Mr. Murphy, the owner, would always reach into the change cup on the counter and give me a nickel for the Chiclets gum machine by the front door.

"They were losing business," Dad continued, tracing his finger around the ridges on the coffee cup lid. "What choice did they have? Eventually they had to face the facts, and that meant closing the store and letting all of us go."

I stared, still shocked. "The whole store is closed for good? Forever?"

"Yep."

"What are you going to do? Have you got another job?" Even as the words left my mouth, I knew this was a completely stupid question. Of course he didn't have another job yet. For years, all he had done was sell shoes. How many shoe salesman jobs were floating around out there in the world?

I could picture my mom's expression when she eventually heard the news. Her lips would tighten into a disapproving line. She would take a deep slow breath, as if she was silently counting to ten. "It's always something," she would say finally, staring at the ceiling and sighing. "Always something with your father."

Next, fill in the words: *And that's why we got divorced.* Although my mom never spoke those words out loud, of course. The other unspoken words floating around in the air would be: *Please don't turn out like your dad.*

No chance.

Dad moved his coffee cup to the side and rested his arms on the table. "So here's the deal, Josh," he said, leaning forward and picking up one of the straw paper balls I'd made. He rolled it back and forth between his fingers. "I entered this contest at the mall in June—an Elvis singing contest. I'd just lost my job at Murphy's a few weeks before and I thought what the hell—" He glanced around and lowered his voice. "Heck. I thought what the heck have I got to lose? No job. Nothing else to do, right? So I paid the ten-dollar contest fee, borrowed a black leather jacket from this friend of mine, got some of those stick-on sideburns, and went up there and sang my tail off." He leaned closer and his voice fell to an excited whisper. "I mean, I wasn't half bad, Josh. Really, I wasn't. People clapped pretty hard for me at least and one lady came running up to the stage and kissed me. I mean, I didn't even know this woman! She just wrapped her arms around me and planted one right—"

"Okay, Dad, I get it." *Jeesh, this was way more than I needed to know.*

"Well, here's the thing," my dad continued. "I actually won the contest. Can you believe that? Jerry Denny. FIRST place. Two hundred fifty bucks." He snapped his fingers together. "Just like that. For singing ONE song. Two hundred and fifty dollars. That would've been three days of work at Murphy's. Three days of lugging stacks

19

of shoeboxes around and saying nice things about people's stinking feet. So," he said, leaning back and smiling. "What do you think?"

I wasn't sure what to think, except that I promised myself I would not set foot in Chicago's Summerland Mall after hearing this story. All I could picture was my dad standing on the mall stage where they put Santa Claus every Christmas—my forty-year-old dad wearing somebody's black leather jacket and trying to twist his hips like Elvis (oh god, did he really twist his hips?) and singing badly and getting kissed at the end by some wacko mall woman.

And what if the purpose of the contest had been to get people to go onstage and make fools of themselves? There were contests like that, did my dad realize that? Maybe the money and applause hadn't been for being the best, it had been for being Chicago's biggest joke. . . .

I glanced over at my dad's proud grin. Even the parrots on his shirt looked like they were stupidly smiling. A hollow feeling started burrowing a place in my stomach. "I'm gonna get something to eat," I said, standing up suddenly. "I'm hungry."

"Sure, sure"—Dad waved his hand toward the counter—"get yourself a snack. We'll have dinner later at home."

I took a long time to order. While I was standing there, I noticed an overweight, greasy-haired guy about my dad's age working at the take-out window. Which made me think about my dad serving burgers and fries at McDonald's someday, if he couldn't find another shoe store job.

"Whenever you're ready," the counter girl kept saying, giving me an annoyed look for taking up space. Even though McDonald's in Chicago are the same as the ones in Boston, I stared at the menu choices like I was reading them for the first time. I couldn't seem to decide on anything. My mind jumped from one thought to the next— Elvis, my dad, Mr. Murphy's store closing, my mom in Florida, my grandma in the hospital with her broken hip—and my eyes kept moving back to the greasy-haired guy who was handing people's orders through the take-out window. How had he gotten there? I wondered. Did he go from selling sneakers to flipping burgers?

The counter girl glared at me. "Ready yet?"

"Strawberry milk shake," I answered finally, even though I didn't really want a milk shake and I never order strawberry.

5. Shaking Things Up

When I got back to the booth, my dad slid a small card across the table. "Here. This is what I wanted you to see."

Printed in gold letters on the white business card were the words JERRY DENNY AS THE KING. FOR BOOKING INFORMATION, CALL . . .

Below was my dad's phone number.

Dad leaned back in the booth, smiling like he had just won the lottery or something. "So what's your reaction?"

"To what?" I replied, loudly squeaking my straw up and down in the milk shake cup, as if this would cover up the sound of what my dad was going to say next, which I had already guessed.

"About me being Elvis, you know, as a way to earn a living. Just temporarily. I used to sing in that band in college when your mom and I were dating. I only gave it up when we moved here to Chicago and I never got around to finding another band. I'm not that bad a singer. You've heard me before—am I a bad singer?"

I've heard my dad sing in exactly three places: the car, birthday parties, and baseball games. He can sing the national anthem better (and louder) than most people, I've noticed. And he's the one who usually starts off "Happy Birthday" when nobody else wants to sing. But that doesn't make you Elvis.

I've also seen a few out-of-focus pictures of my dad and his college band, the Fifth Street Players. Picture guys with really big '80s hair who look more like static electricity experiments than singers.

Still squeaking the straw up and down, I tried to figure out what to answer. "I think people won't really get it." This was the nicest, vaguest advice I could come up with. "They might think it's a little weird that you want to pretend to be Elvis," I added. "As a job."

A hurt look flickered across my father's face. "Do you really think it's weird?"

I don't know why, but the fact that my dad didn't seem to have a clue about why this was a bad idea was beginning to bug me. How many adults did he see walking around with parrot shirts and triangle sideburns calling themselves the King?

"It's not exactly normal." The words came out of my

mouth more sarcastically than I planned, and the parrot feathers looked ruffled as Dad stood up.

"That's okay. Everybody's entitled to their own opinion, I guess." Swiping his business card from the middle of the table and jamming it in the front pocket of his shirt, he kept on talking to me over his shoulder. "I just thought you and I could have some fun with this idea while you were staying here. I figured maybe you'd want to help out at some of my gigs—you know, work the sound equipment or something. But if you aren't up for that, hey, it's your choice. You're getting old enough to make your own choices these days, I guess." He pushed open the door of the McDonald's with one hand. It swung back hard and smacked into mine as if my dad was saying, *Take that for hurting my feelings.*

Really, though—help out at his gigs? I stared at the smirking parrots on my dad's back as we stepped out into the hot blacktop sunshine. It would have been hysterical if it was a joke, and I knew if I called my buddy Brian in Boston and told him the whole story he would probably fall off his pool deck laughing. I could hear his voice: *You're freaking kidding me . . . no way . . . your dad is doing what?* But of course I would never tell something like that to Brian—or to any of my friends in Boston, for that matter.

Once we got in the car, Dad pretended to ignore the

topic of Elvis altogether. He tuned the radio to the Chicago Cubs game. They were losing by eight runs. Since I didn't know many of the Cubs players, except for an outfielder who was traded from Boston (know that feeling), it was hard to make myself care.

As the crowded neighborhoods and rusty factories of Chicago skimmed by the car windows, my dad tried to make conversation. He asked me about school and soccer and even—this was stretching it—the weather in Boston. I could tell he was trying hard to get back on the right foot with me after our bad start.

Note: Getting off to a bad start with each other is pretty normal for us.

When we pulled up to my dad's house, it was the seventh-inning stretch and the score was such a joke the announcers had stopped giving it. My dad flicked off the radio and pointed at the house and yard through the windshield. "Notice anything different?"

At first, I didn't get what he was talking about. Things looked pretty much the same as always. My dad lives on a street called Oakmont in one of the older parts of Chicago. It's one of those city neighborhoods where all of the houses look like they were made with the same house cookie cutter. The ones in his neighborhood are white bungalows with curved metal awnings over their small front porches. The awnings seem to come in one of three colors: black, green, or rusty white. A lot of the windows have awnings over them, too. It must be a Chicago thing.

My dad's house is usually easy to spot because it's the one with the yard that looks most in need of mowing. Sometimes, there are one or two leftover Christmas decorations still on display. Like plastic candy canes or one of those mechanical reindeer with a head that goes up and down. Even in August.

But this time, I could see the Christmas decorations were gone. And the lawn was mowed in neat diagonal stripes, almost like a miniature baseball field. A basket of straggly purple flowers hung from the front porch.

"Looks different, huh?" My dad nodded at the yard as we tugged the suitcases out of the car. "Been trying to find things to keep myself busy now that I'm home all day. Can't sit around doing nothing, you know."

When he pushed open the front door, a bleach-smelling tidal wave came rolling out, so I could tell that cleaning was one of the things he'd been doing. "Check out what's new in your bedroom," Dad said excitedly, pointing down the small hallway.

After seeing my bedroom, I could tell my dad was doing his best to be different (better) on this visit. I wasn't sure if it was me turning thirteen or what, but the embarrassing *Empire Strikes Back* bedspread that had been on the bed since I was about seven was finally gone.

*May the Force be with you, old bedspread, wherever you
are. . . .*

Above the bed, Dad had put up two new posters.
They were those inspirational-message-type ones, which I
wasn't crazy about, but I didn't say anything. One had the
word SUCCESS and the other PERSEVERANCE. The pictures
on them weren't bad, though—a crowd of running shoes
crossing a finish line in one, and a kayaker going through
some kind of orange Popsicle–colored canyon in the other.

Looking around, I also noticed that the room was
clean. Everything wasn't covered in a layer of dust like it
usually was. When I was younger, I always used to imagine that nobody touched the room between my visits and
even the air was kept sealed inside like King Tut's tomb
until I opened the door the next time.

"What do you think?" My dad thumped a suitcase
down on the bed.

"It's good, thanks," I said, being cautiously nice,
but not overly nice. I didn't want my dad thinking a new
bedspread and a few posters would suddenly turn me into
his best buddy.

But he kept trying. He had bought a bucket of KFC
fried chicken for dinner, which was one of my personal
favorites, and here was the real shocker—he'd made a
batch of brownies, too. "Ta-da," he announced, whipping
the foil cover off the brownies. "Double chocolate fudge,

made by Chef Jerry Denny himself. Who woulda thought this old man could cook?"

While he was tossing everything onto the table—fried chicken, mashed potatoes, rolls, corn, brownies—I noticed he hadn't set a place for me. There was only one for himself. This was typical. My dad spent most of the year without having me around, so it was probably easy to forget me when I was there. *Josh? Josh who?* But I guess part of me still thought he should feel guilty about forgetting.

"You didn't set anything for me," I pointed out as I pulled my own plate from the cupboard.

Dad waved his hand at the table. "Go ahead. I'm not eating. I'll have the leftovers later."

"Later?"

"Got a gig tonight."

A gig? I guess up to this point, I didn't really get the fact that my dad was serious. Okay, I could see that maybe he was serious about wanting to start a singing business, but I didn't expect many people would seriously hire him to perform as Elvis Presley. This was Chicago, not Las Vegas. And if it wasn't for the new sideburns and the dyed hair, my father would look almost nothing like Elvis.

Dad leaned forward and squinted at the tiny clock on his old stove. "In fact, crap, is that the time? I gotta get ready." He shoved one last pan onto the table with a metallic clang. "If you need anything, give me a holler upstairs." As he was going up the steps, he called out to me, "When I come back down, be prepared to meet the King!"

Looking at it later, this should have been my first clue that my dad had already decided pretending to be a famous dead person was a whole lot more fun than being an ordinary living one.

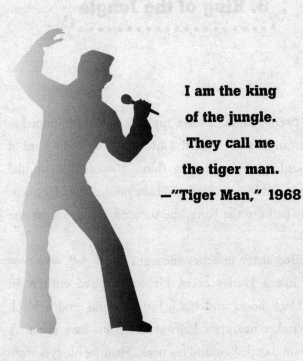

**I am the king
of the jungle.
They call me
the tiger man.
—"Tiger Man," 1968**

6. King of the Jungle

About twenty minutes later, my dad suddenly jumped—and I mean *jumped*—into the kitchen doing some kind of knee-bending, arm-swinging thing. I swear if there had been any food in my mouth, I'd have needed the Heimlich.

"Say hello to the King," he shouted, balancing on one knee.

I stared at the unbelievable sight of my dad, who now looked like a Harley biker. He was dressed entirely in black: black boots and black leather pants and a black leather jacket unzipped halfway down his bare chest. A gold chain dangled around his neck. Shading his eyes were huge gold-framed sunglasses. And his face was orange. Seriously, it was.

Note to Dad: As far as I know, the real Elvis didn't have an orange face.

"How's my costume?" he said, stretching out his arms

32

to give me the full effect, which showed off enough of his forty-year-old chest hair to make me feel uncomfortable. "It's the 1968 Comeback Special outfit."

"Comeback Special?"

"It's what Elvis wore for his first big television show after the army and Hollywood. So whaddaya think? Can the King bring it home, son, huh?" My dad pumped his arm around in a circle and accidentally hit two plastic fish magnets, which went flying off the refrigerator.

"Bring what home?"

"It's a saying, Josh—you know, make it happen, make it work." My dad gave me a frustrated look, as if I wasn't reacting the way he wanted. "That's okay, just forget it." He stood up slowly, creaking upward on one black leather knee, and came over to the table. I could see now that the orange color was makeup. Way too much makeup. Not only that, but his palms looked like a ballpoint pen had leaked all over them.

"What's on your hands?"

"Lyrics." Dad held out his left hand, showing me how the blue smudges were words crowded into every spare inch of skin. There were even words written on each of his fingers. "All the ones I keep forgetting." He laughed and wiped away a trickle of sweat coming down his face.

Note to Dad: Please tell me you don't actually go onstage with the lyrics written on your *hands*.

33

"So why don't you come along tonight, Josh, and see what my show's like? I promise I won't embarrass you or anything. It'll be a good time. I'm just doing a little restaurant gig down the road. Whaddaya say?"

I think my dad really expected me to come with him. But there was no way. *No way.* Not after seeing the lyrics on his hands. And his orange face. And the ridiculous gold sunglasses. I couldn't believe he actually went out in public, looking like he did. What did people say when they saw him at traffic lights? Or gas stations?

My dad started down the hall, talking half like Elvis and half like Jerry Denny. "You're gonna have to hurry up, though, because the King is already running—crap—twenty minutes late."

I called out from the kitchen that I didn't really feel like going with him. That I just wanted to watch TV and hang out at home instead.

"You sure?" My dad's muffled voice continued down the hall, along with a lot of thumping and banging, which I could only assume was coming from things he was attempting to carry out the door. "It's gonna be fun. . . ."

"That's okay, thanks."

"Your choice," he answered, and pulled the front door closed with a house-shaking thud. After he left, everything was weirdly silent. The words "Elvis has left the building" went through my head. The strong smell of my dad's hair spray, or aftershave, or whatever he was wearing still drifted in the air. An empty guitar case was sitting smack in the middle of the hallway. The house had the feeling of being suddenly abandoned. Or maybe it was me who had the feeling of being abandoned.

Sitting in the kitchen staring at the Colonel's happy face on the chicken bucket, I tried to decide if what had happened since I'd arrived in Chicago belonged in the category of THINGS TO TELL MY MOM or THINGS TO KEEP TO MYSELF. This was a gray area for all divorced kids. It was like being a two-way mirror: you could reveal some important stuff between houses, but not everything.

From past experiences, I had learned it was not a good idea to share anything related to my parents' current dating life, anything related to presents or money they had given to me, or anything that made one house or parent seem better than the other.

But the fact that my dad had lost his job at Murphy's Shoes and was setting out on some crazy course to become Jerry Denny as the King seemed like something my mom ought to know. And how many nights was he really going to be gone on these "gigs"? I mean, I didn't mind having some time on my own. I kind of liked the fact that my dad usually gave me more space than my mom, who tapped on my bedroom door about once an hour to make sure I hadn't been abducted by aliens or knocked unconscious by kidnappers. But sitting around Chicago by myself for a few months wasn't my idea of a good time, either.

When a phone call interrupted the silence a few minutes later, I have to admit I was pretty relieved to hear my mom's normal voice on the other end. At least she hadn't turned into Elvis or any other rock-and-roll legend, as far as I could tell.

"Are you unpacked and settled in yet?"

I told her yes, because my mom is a worrier and if I told her the truth—that my clothes were still jammed in my suitcases and would probably stay that way for a couple more days—I knew I would get a long lecture on taking care of my stuff, and I wasn't really into listening to all that. Plus, if I kept my clothes packed up, there was the slim chance that maybe I could still leave Chicago.

"And how's your dad?" she asked, which was typically the second Mom question. She said it that way every time. *Your* dad. Emphasis on the *your*. As if he was somebody she had no connection to and didn't know very well. This always seemed bizarre to me since she had once been *married* to the guy, for cripes sake. My dad wasn't much different when he talked about her.

"He's okay," I said, knowing this was the perfect opportunity to tell my mom about Murphy's closing and Dad's Elvis business. I could start by saying how a few things had changed since the last time I'd seen Dad—and finish by telling her it was probably a good idea if I didn't stay in Chicago. That it would be better for everybody if I came to Florida instead.

However, unloading all of this news on my mom in the first thirty seconds of our phone call didn't seem right, either. So I decided to wait a little longer, hoping maybe the topic would happen to come up on its own. If my mom asked me how work had been going for my dad, for instance, I'd have no choice but to tell her the truth, right?

But she had already moved on to another subject.

Chance number one, gone.

I could hear an odd waver in my mom's voice as she told me how my grandma was not as good as she had hoped. Mom had taken a flight to Florida just a few hours after I'd left for Chicago, and this was the first time she'd seen my grandma since her accident. "She's still in the hospital and can't do much of anything for herself. She's in a lot of pain, I'm afraid," my mom said, sounding worried.

It was hard to picture my grandma in the hospital. The last time I'd seen her, she was perfectly fine. Mom and I had spent a week in June visiting her at the Shadyside Villas trailer park. Every night, she would ease into her blue recliner at six-thirty to watch the evening news, and afterward we would go with her on her "walkabout," as she liked to call it: two laps of the trailer park at a pace that felt like being in a slow-motion movie to me.

Then the three of us would sit around the picnic table on my grandma's porch playing Hearts or Knockout or just Solitaire if nobody was up for a real game. Grandma had taught me to play Solitaire as a little kid, when I could hardly hold the cards, let alone shuffle them. Now I took a pack of cards everywhere I went. "Everybody needs a constructive way to pass the time," my grandma often said, which I think was a not-so-subtle reference to my grandpa George, who had passed his time by smoking and drinking too much, I guess. He'd died way before I was born, so I'd never met him—which my mom said was probably a good thing. Evidently, he wasn't a shining role model in general.

"Grandma asked about you," Mom continued. "She felt bad that you had to leave your school and your friends in Boston, but I told her not to worry—you are the kind of kid who can adjust to anything. Unlike your mom, who frets about everything, right?" She laughed uneasily, as if this was true—which it was. "I told your grandma that maybe this visit with your dad will turn out to be a good chance for you to spend more time with him, now that you're getting older and can do more things together."

And right there, I knew my best chance to say something about Dad had totally evaporated. What was I supposed to say after that? *Hey, Mom, did you know Dad is now pretending to be Elvis? Or Mom, guess what? Dad lost his job*

and he's broke, so he's singing at some restaurant tonight and I'm eating a bucket of cold KFC chicken by myself.

Even asking if I could come to Florida didn't seem like a good idea. I could tell by the wobbly sound of my mom's voice that she was totally stressed out, and I knew she was probably making up her Post-it note lists like there was no tomorrow: THINGS TO BUY FOR GRANDMA, DOCTORS TO TALK TO, PEOPLE TO CALL, ERRANDS TO RUN. . . .

"You're pretty quiet," she said, as if suspecting something.

"Just tired," I answered.

"Everything's okay there?"

"Yeah, fine."

"Your dad will get you signed up for school, right?"

"I guess."

It was like playing twenty questions over the phone. I wasn't sure what I was trying to hide, and my mom didn't have any clue what she was trying to find out. And so it pretty much ended in a draw, with my mom saying she would call back in a day or two with an update on my grandma. "Be good for your dad," she finished, which was what she always said, even though I was no longer five.

Of course, once I got off the phone and realized what I'd done, I decided I was the biggest moron on the planet. There had been so many chances to say something, even to give my mom a small hint, and I'd said zip. Zero.

Who was I protecting? I wondered. My dad? My mom? Myself? Definitely not myself—otherwise I wouldn't be stuck in an empty house in Chicago eating cold mashed potatoes that had hardened into something resembling crusty kindergarten paste. I would have been hopping on the next plane to Florida.

I tried to cut some of the brownies, which turned out to be burned to the bottom of the pan. When they wouldn't come out, I finally gave up and started scraping them off the bottom with a fork and picking up the crumbs with my fingers. Then the phone rang again. It was a call for my dad, and when I told the woman my name, she laughed. *Why is the name Josh Greenwood funny to you?* I wanted to ask, but I didn't because it was my dad's house and his phone.

"Just tell your dad that Viv called, honey," the woman replied cheerfully.

As if the day hadn't already had enough bad surprises— my dad hadn't mentioned a word about knowing anybody named Viv. And I hated being called "honey."

7. I Ain't Askin' Much of You

"Who's Viv?" I asked at breakfast the next morning, even though I knew it probably wasn't the right time to be throwing one question after another at my dad. Sitting across from me, he seemed kind of worn-out. In the blinding morning sunlight coming through his kitchen window, I could see patches of razor stubble on his chin and his eyes looked puffy and tired. He'd gotten home from his show at about midnight. I'd heard him trip over the guitar case in the darkness.

"Viv?" my dad repeated, his voice hoarse. He took a big swallow of coffee. "What about her?"

"She called last night."

"Oh yeah? Okay. Thanks." My dad took a large bite of toast and acted as if this was completely uninteresting news. "I'm sure we'll run into her eventually," he said, chewing slowly.

From the tone of his voice, I couldn't tell if Viv was a new girlfriend or not. I'd met quite a few of my dad's girlfriends over the years. None of them had impressed me very much, and to be honest, there were several I had completely hated: the second-grade teacher with the frizzed-out hair (Linda? Lynne?) who always asked me endless school questions. The ditzy insurance lady who drove her huge car over every curb when she turned a corner: "Oops, sorry for that little bump in the backseat!" And who could forget KPG—Killer Perfume Girlfriend? (I couldn't remember her real name.) Her choking perfume would linger in the house for days after she left, like a toxic death cloud.

"Hey, speaking of people"—my dad snapped his fingers, as if he was trying to change the subject—"I've got somebody for you to meet. Once you finish up your breakfast, I'll take you down the street and introduce you to my new friend Gladys."

Fortunately, Gladys turned out to be a very elderly neighbor of my dad's—not a potential girlfriend. She lived in a house with rusty white awnings, five doors down the street. A ceramic goose with a blue bonnet sat next to her front door. Even though it was almost noon when we knocked, the lady who answered the door was still dressed in her bathrobe. This made me pretty uncomfortable, although my dad didn't seem fazed at all. "Can I help you, gentlemen?" the woman said, peering at us uncertainly through the screen door. Her hair was an odd shade of yellowish white, and the way it was standing up in clumps all over her head reminded me of the stuffing coming out of a couch.

"How are you doing today, Gladys?" my dad said loudly.

The lady blinked, leaned closer, and then beamed a wide smile of recognition. "Why, if it isn't my boyfriend Elvis!" she exclaimed. Did everybody in Chicago know about my dad being Elvis? She pushed open the screen door. "Come in, come in, I'm not at my best this morning, but do come in."

"Gladys, this is Josh," my dad said, nodding in my direction as we stepped through the door. The lady reached out one of her trembling, bird wing hands to shake mine. "It's a pleasure, young man. I don't know how you folks find the time to keep an old lady company, I really don't, but it's a pleasure, that's for sure. I always look forward to a visit by Elvis."

Right then I had the strange feeling that maybe Gladys actually believed my father was Elvis. The real Elvis. Mr. Pelvis himself. I glanced over at my dad. Did he have that sense, too? But he was already following the old lady as she padded slowly down the hall in her pink slippers.

"Are you hungry? Can I get you boys something to eat?" she said when we got to the kitchen, which smelled like burnt toast and stale coffee. Looking around, I knew my mom would've had a fit at the mess: pots and pans overflowing from the sink and a table covered with old newspapers, dirty dishes, and stacks of mail. The lady began pushing the junk to one side of the table, as if clearing a space for us.

"It looks like you forgot to clean up from dinner last night, Gladys," my dad said in a half-joking voice, "and the night before, too." A pan of congealed chicken soup still sat on top of the stove. *Gross.* He held up the two newspapers we had picked up from her driveway on our way in. "And you didn't want today's papers, either, I guess."

Gladys waved her hand in the air nonchalantly. "I can't be bothered with all that."

This lady was definitely senile, or losing her mind, or something, I decided. I had to admit it made me kind of nervous to be around older people who were like that— who were not *all there*, I mean. There were some people at Shadyside Villas who would shout things from their porches like, "Did you see my husband while you were out walking this evening?" My grandma would lean closer to me and whisper under her breath, "Her husband's been dead for ten years, isn't that a pity?" And then she'd shout

44

back to the person, "No, I didn't, dear, but if I do, I'll be sure to let you know." I always tried not to think about my grandma becoming that way someday.

"Gladys makes my scarves for me," my dad explained, flopping down in one of the chairs as if he was planning to stay awhile. I didn't move from where I stood, leaning against the doorway, hoping he would get the clue that I didn't want this to be a long visit.

"And I sewed a few more yesterday," Gladys said as she shuffled out of the room. "You just stay there, dear, and I'll get them for you."

Note to Dad: It's August. Not exactly scarf weather yet.

But Gladys returned wearing an entire scarf rainbow around her neck. At least that's what it looked like. Over the collar of her robe, she had draped a bunch of shiny silk scarves: yellow, pale blue, red, and a few purple ones. "Don't I look lovely, boys?" she exclaimed, holding her arms out and turning around slowly so the ends of the scarves fluttered in the air like crepe paper streamers.

Second note to Dad: Please tell me you aren't really going to wear these scarves. You're just being nice to an old lady, right?

"A few weeks ago, I was telling Gladys how I needed a few scarves to hand out at my Elvis shows," Dad said, reaching down to pick up a yellow one that had slipped off

Gladys's shoulders and fallen onto the floor. "Because during his shows, Elvis would give them away to people in his audience."

Apparently, Elvis liked to use a scarf to wipe his face or his neck or his armpits during a song (seriously) and then he'd hand the scarf to some lady in the crowd, who would act like she'd just received a million dollars from him instead of a sweaty old piece of silk. "Hard to believe, but true," Dad said, nodding.

Gladys laughed in her creaky-hinge kind of way. "And I told him, 'Why, I have this old sewing machine just sitting in my spare bedroom collecting dust. It wouldn't be any trouble at all to make your scarves.'" She smiled as she draped the rainbow of scarves over the back of my dad's chair and patted his shoulder with her hand. "Who would've thought I'd be sewing for Elvis at my age?"

Incredibly, my dad still didn't say anything at this point. He didn't correct her. Didn't tell her he was Jerry Denny, former shoe salesman. Instead, he laughed and said in his fake Elvis drawl, "Well, let's see if the King can help you get this kitchen back in shape, ma'am."

When we finally left Gladys's house after spending more than an hour straightening her filthy kitchen and putting the dishes with the dried crud in the dishwasher, I didn't even wait until we got to the end of her driveway before the words started coming out of my mouth, fast and furious. "What was THAT all about?" I spouted out first, because it was the only reasonable thing I could think of to say at that moment without getting into the specifics of what had been totally wrong about the whole situation.

"What was what all about?" My dad calmly reached down to yank up a straggly weed from a crack in the drive-way concrete.

"Why'd you keep letting that lady call you Elvis?" I gestured in the direction of Gladys's house, where she was still standing at the door. "She thinks that's who you really are."

My dad laughed in that annoying way of his—as if he thought everything I was saying was just one big joke. "No need to get so upset, bud," he said, draping an arm across my shoulders. "When a friend of mine introduced me to Gladys a month or so ago because I was looking for some-body to make some scarves, I tried to explain to her how I just pretend to be Elvis and wear a costume and makeup and stuff. But then, in the middle of explaining, I decided—so what? Maybe thinking I'm the real Elvis makes her happy. And if it makes her happy, why ruin it?"

I tugged my shoulders out from underneath my father's trying-to-be-your-buddy arm. "I just don't get it."

My dad gave an annoyed sigh. "What don't you get, Josh?"

"Why you're trying to be *freakin' Elvis,* and why we

47

had to help clean that lady's kitchen," I said under my breath, just loud enough to be heard.

"Well then why don't you tell me what we should be doing, Josh?" My dad's voice was getting an impatient edge to it. "Because I don't seem to have it right, do I? I thought I was a shoe salesman. Spent fifteen years of my life in some lousy store selling high heels and sneakers, and then the place goes broke, bankrupt, overnight, and I've gotta figure out who I am all over again at the age of forty, which isn't a whole lot of fun, I'll tell you that."

Since I could see all I was getting was a lecture, I shut up and concentrated on staring at the air, as if the molecules just in front of my nose were completely fascinating.

My dad kept on talking. He went into a long story about how Elvis always cared about ordinary people, even when he was famous. "You could be a complete stranger and he'd turn around and give you a Cadillac if he felt like it," my dad continued. "I read about somebody who was just admiring Elvis's car in the parking lot and Elvis came over and told the person, 'Lady, this one's mine, but I'll take you to the showroom and buy a new one for you,' and he bought her a brand-new car. Didn't even know who she was! Gave her an eleven-thousand-dollar Cadillac," my dad finished.

I had no idea what free Cadillacs had to do with washing Gladys's dishes or my dad losing his job at Murphy's, but I didn't say anything.

"Gladys is just a lonely old lady living by herself, Josh. The only family she's got is some worthless nephew who never shows up. We spent an hour helping her to clean her kitchen. How hard was that?" Dad bumped his elbow into my side. "And as Elvis would say, 'Hey baby'"—he pretended to hold a microphone out to me—"'I ain't askin' much of you. . . .'"

All this aggravation ain't
satisfactioning me.
—"A Little Less Conversation," 1968

8. The Domino Effect

Elvis was one problem. School was another. Before coming to Chicago, I'd been to only two schools in my life, both of them in Boston. Which is why I'd been dreading the whole possibility of going to a new one, even if it was only for a few months. What if it turned out to be one of those tough schools—the kind of place they show on the evening news where kids get clobbered by school bus thugs?

I held on to the slim hope that maybe my dad would completely forget about enrolling me in seventh grade like he forgets his car keys, his sunglasses, his cell phone, and his mind on a daily basis. If I was lucky, maybe I could spend four months in Chicago free and clear of teachers and homework. Unfortunately, I'd only been at his house for about a week when he brought up the subject. We were eating lunch one afternoon and he said, "I need to buy some more milk and get you signed up for school, don't I?"

In case you're wondering about the connection between buying milk and enrolling me in school, it turns out that the Dairy Barn grocery store where my dad buys his milk just happens to be across the street from the school. So if we hadn't run out of milk, would he have totally forgotten about signing me up for seventh grade?

Possibly.

However, before I set foot in any school building with him, I had already decided he was going to make a few changes. Like wearing a hat. And socks with his sneakers. And a normal, non-parrot (or any other type of wildlife) shirt. I wasn't taking any chances that somebody would see my dad's Elvis hair or his weird clothes and start rumors about me before the school year even got started. I could hear it now: *You know that new kid? His dad thinks he's Elvis. Ya-hah-hah. . . .*

Talk about an easy target.

"You gonna wear your Cubs cap?" I suggested as we were leaving for the Great School Sign-up Experience the next morning. Except for his hair, everything else about my dad looked fairly normal that day.

"Something wrong with my hair?" he said, reaching up to check.

"It's sunny outside."

My dad glanced out the window at the sky, which was totally cloudy. "No, I'll be fine."

"It's supposed to get sunny." I knew my voice sounded desperate.

My dad gave me an odd look, but he pulled his Cubs cap out of the jumble of coats and shoes in his hall closet and tugged it on his head before we left. "How's that?"

"Great." Actually, you could still see the bottom edges of the sideburns, but they didn't draw as much attention under the hat. I figured the other advantage I had was the fact that my last name was different than his, so people probably wouldn't make the connection between our names. Normally, I wasn't too crazy about my last name, which was also my mom's last name: Greenwood. Sounds like a golf course. But at least it would take people longer to figure out that Jerry Denny, the winner of the Summerland Mall Elvis competition, was related to me.

As we pulled up to my new school, I was surprised by its size. The sign said Charles W. Lister Intermediate. Different wings of the school spread out in various directions like a giant game of dominoes, and we had a hard time finding which part actually held the main office. After wandering around a bunch of empty, squeaky-clean hallways, we finally spotted the main office across from a large plaque showing Charles W. Lister's face. In bronze.

At the top of the plaque, it said CHARLES W. LISTER (1851–1927). At the bottom were the words PIONEER—EDUCATOR—LEADER—FRIEND.

While we were waiting in the office, I started thinking about the various words that might go on a plaque about me: *Josh Greenwood: friend—soccer player—thirteen-year-old.* What else? I couldn't come up with anything besides *divorced kid*, which didn't seem like the right kind of phrase for a plaque. And maybe it was better not to have a label that would go on a plaque anyway. There were a lot of bad ones out there: brain, loser, geek, wacko, freak. . . .

"And who's this?" a voice asked.

My dad tugged on my arm, and we walked over to the tall counter where a handwritten sign said ALL VISITORS MUST SIGN IN. The secretary was a blond lady who looked like she had spent way too much time in the sun over the summer. Her skin reminded me of the color of those boiled Atlantic lobsters they sell in Boston grocery stores.

"This is my son Joshua Aaron Greenwood," my dad began. "His mother and I are divorced, and he's been living in Massachusetts for the past eight years. . . ."

Note to Dad: You don't need to tell this lady our entire life story.

But my dad didn't seem to get my subliminal message. He went through the complete medical description of my grandma's injury and explained how I would be staying with him for the next few months or so. When he began telling how he had recently lost his job at Murphy's Shoes, I could see he was getting dangerously close to bringing up Elvis. I glanced around the office, desperately searching for something to ask a question about. There was a large trophy sitting on the windowsill, and I asked the lady what it was for.

"Our show choir," she answered, giving me a hopeful look. "We have an excellent music program here. Do you sing?"

I could feel a red warmth creeping slowly up my neck as I told the lady no, I played soccer and baseball back in Boston—knowing, of course, that my dad was just waiting for the chance to jump in and announce how he was the first-place winner of the Elvis singing competition at the Summerland Mall.

However, by some miracle, it turned out that the secretary's son played the same two sports as me. Thankfully, she launched into a long story about her son's problems with his baseball coach, and by the time she was finished, the whole topic of singing had been left safely behind.

As my dad stood at the counter filling out the endless school forms, I tried to avoid being noticed by the kids who walked in and out of the office. Even though it was the middle of August, the building was full of kids who must have been there for sports or summer school. Whenever the loud *thwap, thwap, thwap* of their flip-flops came toward the counter where we were standing, I turned slightly to one side and pretended to be studying an important-looking piece of paper taped near my left elbow, titled MANDATORY FIRE EVACUATION PROCEDURES.

In between reading useful evacuation advice like DON'T PANIC, PROCEED TO THE NEAREST EXIT, I also tried to check out what people were wearing, since I didn't want my clothes to scream "weirdly dressed new kid" on the first day. My usual school style in Boston could be summed up as jeans and T-shirts in some shade of brown, blue, black, or, occasionally, orange because it was my Boston school color. Nothing with stripes or prints. Ever. Which always drove my mom crazy. From what I saw the guys wearing at Charles Lister, I would fit in just fine.

After the paperwork was finished, the secretary handed us a Lister Intermediate School bumper sticker and a gold metallic folder with Charles W. Lister's portrait on the front. *Pioneer—Educator—Leader—Friend.* "Welcome to Lister." She smiled. "We're glad to have you here, Joshua."

Note to secretary: I am not glad.

As we left, the realization that I was actually going to be walking through the doors of this place in about two weeks began to sink in. My stomach felt slightly sick—

like when you are going up to the plate in baseball and there are already two outs and you have the feeling you are about to be number three. That's the way my stomach felt. Nervously sick.

"You want to take a drive past the old Murphy's building?" my dad suggested. "See what's happening there?"

"Sure, okay."

Anything to get my mind off starting over at a new school, but I didn't say that.

9. Jerry's Blue Suede Shoes

Murphy's Shoes was on State Street, in a small city block of old brick buildings and neighborhood businesses that looked as if they had been there for the last hundred years. On the corner was a pharmacy called Kent's Drugstore, which always had large and rather scary advertising signs taped to its windows: HALF-PRICE HEARING AIDS, WHEELCHAIRS, BLOOD PRESSURE CHECKS, and COLD RX.

Harpy's Video came after the pharmacy, followed by a little music store with a dusty-looking guitar display in the front window. Murphy's Shoes was the fourth, and last, store in the block. My dad drove by it slowly and parked in one of the empty spots out front. The big white-and-green Murphy's sign was still hanging on the building, but the windows were covered with brown paper and a thick chain was wrapped through the two door handles. It seemed strange to see the building locked up, looking as if somebody had recently died there.

My dad rested his arms across the steering wheel and squinted through the windshield. "Doesn't seem like anybody has done much with the place yet, does it?" He was silent for a few minutes, just staring at the building. "Lotsa good memories there, right?" he sighed, shaking his head. "Still miss that old place."

Sometimes I couldn't figure out my dad at all. One minute, he could be going on and on about how much he liked being Elvis, and the next minute, he could be talking about how much he missed his job as a shoe salesman. It was another one of the things my mother said was a problem with him. He bounced from one idea to the next. It was hopeless to try and keep up.

"I thought you didn't like selling shoes," I replied, playing with the window button, pushing it up and down.

"I never said that," my dad insisted. "I liked Murphy's. I just wanted to be more of a big shot—you know, running my own store someday."

"Your own store?" I couldn't picture my dad running a store.

Dad tossed his baseball cap into the backseat and rumpled his Elvis hair with his fingers. "Let's get a closer look at the place," he said, jumping out. We walked up to the windows, hoping to see between the sections of brown paper. "You know what I'd call my own place?"

"No," I said, trying to check out if the old Chiclets gum machine was still by the door.

"Blue Suede Shoes," he replied, turning toward me with a big smile. "Isn't that a great name?" He gestured toward the Murphy's sign. "Can't you see it on a big sign right up there? Jerry's Blue Suede Shoes. We could play Elvis songs and the salesmen could wear gold sunglasses and big sideburns. Imagine buying your shoes from Elvis." He grinned. "Wouldn't that be something people would talk about?"

It was a pretty creative idea, I had to admit. Better than going around town singing in shopping malls and restaurants. But how was he going to buy a store without a job?

"How much does Murphy's cost?" I knew this question sounded like something my practical mother would point out. She worked in the accounting department of a big company. Numbers were her thing.

"Too much." My dad laughed. "Way too much for me. But hey, it doesn't hurt to have dreams, right?" He turned away from the windows and glanced down the street. "How about an ice cream?"

We picked up two cones from the little custard stand across the street from Murphy's and sat on the bench outside, eating them and watching the traffic go by. "Probably tough going to a new school, huh?" my dad said.

I took a big bite out of my cone. "Kinda, yeah."

"You'll do fine, don't worry." He paused and I could see a slow grin creeping across his face. "But what was up with all those gold sculptures of that Lister guy, huh? Talk about being in love with your looks." He pretended to copy Charles W. Lister's serious pioneer expression on the school plaque, which was funny, even though I tried not to laugh.

At times like this my dad was all right, you know— kind of like a normal dad. If I closed my eyes, I could almost convince myself this was something we did together all the time—hanging out and eating chocolate-dip ice cream cones, with little blobs of ice cream landing like meteorites around our feet.

10. Trouble

My dad may have believed everything at my new school would work out fine, but I wasn't taking any chances. For my first day at Charles W. Lister, I had three simple rules for myself: 1. Do not say anything stupid. 2. Do not do anything stupid. 3. Do not get lost.

As I got ready for school on the first day, I went over the rules again in my mind. Rule # 3 was going to be the toughest one, I figured, because of the size of the school—if you weren't careful, you could probably wander around the domino hallways for weeks.

I managed to get lost in the first ten minutes.

I was trying to find my first-period class, seventh-grade English, and somehow ended up in the science wing. After circling through a bunch of lab rooms like a lost rat in a maze, I finally spotted a poster of William Shakespeare hanging next to a set of stairs leading to the second floor.

To be lost, or not to be lost: that is the question. . . .

Once I found the right floor and the right classroom, I tried to look as unpanicked as possible as I slid into an empty seat near the wall. Binders and notebooks got shoved under the chairs, so I shoved mine under my chair. Nobody got out their pencils or any other potential writing utensils, so I didn't.

However, I couldn't decide what kind of expression to have on my face. While I wanted to look friendly, I couldn't exactly sit there smiling like a goofball at nothing. For instance, a lot of kids around me were pointing out how the English teacher had some dried white toothpaste stuck in the corner of his lips. Showing I was interested in being included in the toothpaste conversation meant looking at whoever was talking, but I couldn't stare at them for too long, especially if they weren't paying attention to me. And I definitely couldn't smile AND stare, or that would make me a complete loser. So I spent most of my time looking at things that would not look back, such as the ballpoint pen marks on my desk or the inspirational posters tacked up on the bulletin boards: ACHIEVEMENT. EFFORT. IMAGINATION. They reminded me of the ones on my bedroom walls at home. Same idea. Different advice.

When the teacher started taking attendance, I could feel my heart hammering as the *G*s got closer. I hated having my name called by adults. It always made me nervous.

"Joshua Greenwood," the teacher called out, glancing up uncertainly.

"Over here." I only half lifted my arm, trying not to be too eager.

"You're new, yes?"

All of the eyes in the room turned to stare. Imagine being an ape in a zoo with thirty faces pressed up against the glass gawking at you. That's what it felt like.

"Yeah," I answered, trying to lean back a little and suddenly realizing the back of the chair was farther away than I thought, so I was stuck in midlean, with nothing but air behind me.

"Where do you hail from, Josh?" the teacher said, in one of those joking ways some teachers use when talking to kids—which you don't want to get caught in.

I pretended to have no clue what he meant. "Hail?"

When everybody in the room laughed, I knew all of my rules were working out well so far. The teacher gave me a disappointed look, as if he had been hoping for the second coming of Shakespeare and instead got a new kid who didn't even know the meaning of the word "hail."

"Where do you come from is what I meant," he repeated in a clipped voice.

"Boston." I was careful to pronounce it the way my dad did and not "Bahh-ston," which is the way they actually say it where I come from.

"Well, welcome to the Midwest," the teacher finished, as if I was not very welcome, and thankfully moved on to the next person on his list.

One class down.

I only had to repeat I was from Boston five more times, in five more classes. By the time I got to my third class, some of the kids were jumping in to answer the question before I did—which I took as a good sign that I was fitting in okay so far. "He's from Boston," they told the World History teacher, who looked as if she had lived through most of the world's history herself. "Boston, really?" she said, pausing to look over her pair of strange, multicolored bifocals. "How interesting."

The way she said it made everybody snicker around me, and I could tell I was going to be hearing "Boston, reeee-ally, how interesting" for a while, but it could've been worse, I decided.

Lunch went okay, although the cafeteria at Charles W. Lister was huge, way bigger than my school's cafeteria in Boston. It reminded me a lot of Chicago's O'Hare Airport—only with a greasy pizza smell wafting through it and people rushing around carrying flimsy cafeteria trays instead of their carry-on bags.

I had already decided to buy lunch on the first day because I didn't want to risk being the only person at Charles W. Lister walking around with a brown bag dangling from my hand. Unfortunately, the lunch line was located at the far end of the room, and to get there you had to walk through a minefield of kids, teachers, garbage cans, food flying into garbage cans, and custodians pushing around those big gray cafeteria mops. Then, if you made it to the food line in one piece, you had to weave in and out of two sets of doors—one line for ordering, one line for paying—to get your food.

Just to keep from looking totally clueless, I tried to follow whatever the people in front of me were doing. Whatever they ordered, I ordered. Whatever they picked up, I picked up. However, I somehow missed the fact that the cafeteria essentials like plastic silverware and ketchup and mustard were kept on a table *between* the two sets of doors, below a painting of who else: *Good old Charles Lister, Friend of the Condiments.* Since I didn't figure that out on the first day, I had to eat my boiled hot dog and soggy crinkle fries plain.

One of the moments I had been dreading the most was finding a place to sit after I came out of the cafeteria line. Imagine playing musical chairs with a few hundred people and you have to find an open spot before the music ends. Or before everybody starts noticing you are still standing there by yourself, desperately looking for a place to sit.

Foolishly, I'd been hoping somebody might wave their

arm and shout, *Hey, Josh, over here.* Since that didn't happen, I sat at the end of a table of guys who looked fairly normal. The guy who was closest to me glanced over and said, "Hey" when I slid into my seat. He was wearing a Myrtle Beach T-shirt and eating his fries in bunches of three or four at a time. "You came from Boston, right?" he asked me through a mouthful of fries. Actually, he reminded me a little of my friend Brian, who talked to just about everybody. Brian was like a one-man Wal-Mart greeter.

"Yeah," I answered. "A few weeks ago."

"Cool." Another handful of fries disappeared into his mouth. "I've been there twice. I don't remember much about it, though. Just Fenway Park and that old boat they have—what's it called?"

"Old Ironsides."

"Yeah, that was it."

Nobody else at the table seemed to be paying the slightest attention to our conversation, and the Myrtle Beach guy looked like he had run out of Boston things to talk about. He turned back to his friends, who were now jamming wadded-up candy wrappers into a plastic cup, as if he figured he'd been friendly enough. It gave me the chance to scope out other possible places to sit in the cafeteria.

There was a row of vending machines against one wall,

and you could see this was the area where the popular kids sat. Don't ask me how I guessed that from halfway across the room, but I could just tell. In front of the vending machines were several tables of guys in sports jerseys who looked older, and bigger, and more—what was the word . . . important? confident? in charge? (Like if you wanted something from the vending machines, you had to get their approval first.)

I seemed to be sitting in the part of the cafeteria where the average kids had their own little cliques: band kids, computer geeks, runners, wrestlers—you get the picture. Against the farthest wall, nearest the garbage cans, were what I would call the leftovers. They were easy to pick out by their clothes, which did not fit in with anything or anybody around them. I swear one of the guys by the garbage cans looked like he was wearing a real dog collar around his neck, with the leash dangling down his back. *Could that be true?* Somebody else had spiked purple hair. And one girl was wearing orange suspenders and camouflage pants.

Note to self: Do not, under any circumstances, sit near those people.

I polished off the last of my mushy hot dog as the bell rang. Glancing in the direction of the vending machines, I decided that one of my goals over the next few months would be to make it somewhere closer to those tables at

Charles Lister. I sat in the prime seats with my friends in Boston—so why not in Chicago? It couldn't be that difficult, right?

Corn chips and Cheez Doodles, here I come. . . .

Heading back to my locker after my last class, I felt pretty good about how the day had gone. All of my rules had worked out okay: I hadn't done anything stupid, said anything stupid, or gotten totally lost, except for the English class. Nobody had recognized me as being related to the Summerland Mall's first-place Elvis. And I hadn't been beaten up on the school bus or harassed for being the new kid, either. Overall, things hadn't gone too badly, in my opinion.

I was walking down the seventh-grade locker hall, trying to pull the card with my combination out of my pocket, when I noticed the yellow Post-it note stuck to my locker. To be honest, my first thought was my mom and her notes, and my heart jumped a little. I glanced at the kids who were slamming lockers shut around mine, but nobody else seemed to be paying any attention to my yellow note. Or they were pretending not to.

How long had it been there? With my heart pounding nervously, I yanked the message off my locker and held the square of paper on the other side of my textbooks to read it. This was the moment when the whole first day of successes evaporated right in front of my eyes. Scrawled in purple marker on the note were these words:

Welcome to Lister, Josh Greenwood.
Elvisly Yours,

And instead of a name, there was a sneering purple smiley face.

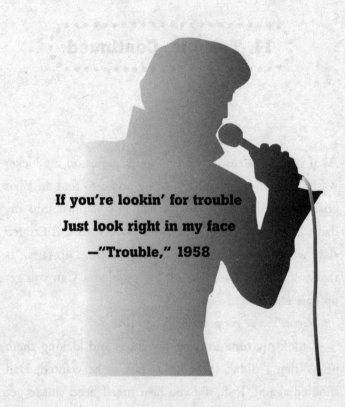

If you're lookin' for trouble
Just look right in my face
—"Trouble," 1958

11. Trouble, Continued

As if getting sarcastic "Elvisly Yours" notes on my locker wasn't bad enough, I had to come home to find an Elvis crisis happening there, too. I had just stepped into my dad's house and closed the front door with a frustrated slam when I heard his voice calling me from upstairs. "Is that you, Josh? Crap, I've got big problems. Can you get up here fast?"

Right. You've got problems? Try mine.

I took my time untying my shoes and kicking them off. When I didn't show up as fast as he wanted, Dad shouted again. "Josh, did you hear me? I need you to get up here quick and help me out."

Upstairs, I found my forty-year-old dad standing in the bathroom covered in an entire bottle of black hair dye. *Yes, I'm being totally serious.* Picture somebody who looks like a character in one of those old black-and-white hor-

74

ror movies: *Jerry Denny and the Attack of the Bathroom Zombies*. He was standing there barefooted with a beige towel wrapped around his waist and Hair Color for Men dripping everywhere. His face, his shoulders, even his feet had hair dye on them. The white linoleum looked like an inkblot test.

The whole scene might have been hysterically funny if I hadn't already been mad. Mad about what had happened at school. Mad that my dad was always doing something embarrassing or stupid. Mad that somebody at Charles Lister had figured out who he was and it wouldn't be long before the entire school knew.

"Read the directions, Josh," my dad said in a frantic voice, jerking his head sideways toward a box sitting on the back of the toilet. His hands were stuck inside two ridiculously large plastic gloves (also covered in black dye), so he couldn't reach for it himself. "How do I get this stuff off?"

I picked up the Hair Color for Men box and skimmed through the words, which seemed to say a lot about how hair color could make you look younger, more successful, less gray, and less self-conscious—but not much about removing it if you screwed up.

"I don't know." I shrugged. "It doesn't give any directions that I could find."

My dad shot me a frustrated look. "Just gimme the

box, Josh. Jeez, I'll read the directions myself." He snatched it out of my hands and more hair dye dripped on the extra towels that were crumpled on the floor around his feet.

"Right here." My dad jabbed his finger at the side of the box. "What does that say? Read that to me." I read the microscopic print about using Vaseline or cold cream to remove the dye if it made contact with the skin. "Check in my medicine cabinet and see if I have any Vaseline." My dad pointed in the direction of the tall wooden cabinet behind the bathroom door. "It'll be in a plastic jar."

I found some in the back of the cabinet after digging around a bunch of shaving cream cans and toilet paper rolls and old shampoo bottles. My dad smeared the stuff on a washcloth and began wiping his face. "I don't know what the heck happened. I must've mixed the formula wrong or something. It just ran all over the place. I thought I could do the color myself—you know, give the sides a little touch-up instead of going back to the salon— but man, was that a mistake."

I leaned against the bathroom doorway, not answering him. There was no way I was going to offer to help with any of the cleanup. Let my dad fix his own mess. I had enough of my own. "Can I leave now?"

"Sure," Dad said, his voice muffled by the washcloth. "School go okay today?"

"Yeah, great." I pulled the bathroom door shut behind me.

When my mom called an hour later, I told her the same thing. "How was your new school?" she asked. I told her it was fine, figuring when I eventually got beat up by the Post-it note people, she'd find out the whole story, right? And if she asked me why I hadn't said something sooner about my dad, I'd tell her I'd been trying to handle my own problems now that I was thirteen and all. Then she would definitely send me a plane ticket to Florida.

Later on, I pulled the yellow note out of my backpack to study it again. Who knew about my dad? And how did they know? I wondered. Had they seen him at the Summerland Mall contest, or did somebody recognize him when we signed up at school? It didn't take a genius to realize that whoever had found out about my dad wouldn't keep the information a secret for very long. It would only be a matter of time before all four hundred seventh graders at Charles Lister knew who I was.

The words on the note were printed in large, bold-looking letters, as if the person writing them hadn't felt any fear about announcing what they knew. But it appeared rushed, too. The dot over the *i* in "Lister" was more like a slash, so it was possible the writer had scribbled the note quickly and slapped it on my locker in a hurry.

I squinted at the smiley face. Would a guy sign a note

with a purple smiley face? It didn't seem like something a guy would do, so maybe that meant the note writer was a girl. But if the smiley face was supposed to be a mocking face—which is how the half-curved mouth looked—then maybe it was a guy.

God, this was crazy.

I crumpled the note in my hand and tossed it toward the garbage can across the room. It missed. I got up and nailed it the second time.

That night, I dreamed about the Charles W. Lister cafeteria. Only, in my dream, my dad's neighbor Gladys was one of the cafeteria ladies and, strangely, a lot of my Boston friends were in line with me. Everything else seemed fairly normal until I came out of the line and began looking for a seat. I was holding my tray, which had turkey and mashed potatoes piled on it, when I realized the room had suddenly gotten quiet and still. I turned around to ask my Boston friend Brian what was going on, and he said, "Look at yourself, freak," and I looked down and realized for the first time that I was wearing a black leather jumpsuit—and I know this sounds pretty disturbing for a thirteen-year-old, but I had black chest hair. Like yarn. *Yarn chest hair.* In the dream, I kept moving from table to table with my lunch tray and my yarn chest hair, and nobody would let me sit down.

12. City Street Blues

The next note appeared on Friday.

All week, I had been checking my locker after each class. This wasn't always easy to do, since most of my classes were at the opposite end of Charles Lister. Clutching my books against my chest, I would leap out of my seat the minute the bell rang and zigzag down the hall the way people do when they have about three minutes to catch a plane. If I got to the point where I could spot my locker in the distance and there were no yellow squares stuck on the green metal, I would do a 180 and race to my next class.

But on Friday, I stopped at my locker right before lunch and there it was—another yellow square stuck crookedly at eye level. My armpits started to prickle as I pulled the note off the locker.

A large peace symbol was scrawled on the paper in

orange marker, along with the same "Elvisly Yours" signature and a smiley face in the corner. Was the peace symbol some kind of warning? Did it have some sinister meaning at Charles Lister that I didn't know about yet?

That afternoon, I decided not to take the school bus home. I wanted time to think, that's what I told myself, but I'll also admit maybe I was feeling slightly paranoid. When you've only been in a new school for a week and people you don't know are obviously watching you and leaving cryptic notes on your locker, I think anybody would feel a little jumpy.

But once I started the couple-mile walk down State Street, lugging two textbooks the size of boulders in my backpack (courtesy of my homework-obsessed World History and Algebra teachers), I felt like an idiot. It had only been a peace symbol, for cripes sake. It wasn't exactly a death threat.

Cars zoomed by me and the air smelled like hot tar and exhaust. I tried to think about Florida instead of focusing on how much farther I had to walk on the shimmering hot sidewalks of Chicago. It was the fifth of September, but the temperature felt like July. I pictured myself in swimming shorts, playing Frisbee on a sunny ocean beach with a cool breeze blowing. If I had gone to school in Florida, that's probably what I would have been doing, right? No Elvis. No hair-dye disasters. No weird

Post-it notes. Just sun and sand. And a cooler full of sodas and chips.

Note to self: Stop it. This isn't helping.

If I made it to the Murphy's Shoes block of State Street, I decided I would stop at Harpy's Video and pick up a can of soda from the machine inside the front door—unless I died of heatstroke before I got there, in which case the whole story of how a peace symbol killed me would probably make the national news.

I was so focused on wrapping my fingers around an ice-cold drink I almost missed the sign taped on the door of Harpy's. As I pushed open the door, I happened to glance down and that's when I saw it. In neatly printed block letters, the sign said: WANTED—DEPENDABLE NIGHT MANAGER. WEEKENDS AND WEEKDAYS. HOURS: 4 P.M. TO MIDNIGHT. GOOD PAY AND BENEFITS. APPLICATIONS INSIDE.

Maybe my decision to walk home had been fate after all.

When I got back to my dad's house after my marathon hike from Charles Lister, he'd already left. Not to go in search of me (although that would have been thoughtful)—he'd left for an Elvis show instead. A note was sitting on the kitchen table underneath a jar of spaghetti sauce and a box of pasta. It said he was performing at a wedding and he'd be back late. Make spaghetti for dinner.

As I dumped my backpack on the kitchen table, I had to admit I was a little disappointed my dad wasn't around because I'd been kinda pumped about showing him the Harpy's application and solving all of his job problems in one easy swipe. The hippie-looking guy who'd been working at the counter of Harpy's Video told me they were desperate to hire somebody.

"Can't take kids, though, because of the hours," he had said as I pulled one of the applications from the pile by the cash register. When I told him it wasn't for me, it was for my dad who had worked at Murphy's before they closed, the guy shook his head. "Murphy's . . . yeah, that was a bummer. Seems like everything's going down the tubes these days. It's the economy," he said, rolling a quarter back and forth across the counter. "Tell your dad to come in and talk to us. I'm sure Harpy would hire him in a heartbeat. He could probably start this weekend if he wanted." But Harpy would have to wait, I guess.

The phone rang while I was in the middle of cooking my spaghetti that night. Standing at the stove, I was feeling like one of those TV chefs: *Cooking with Josh Greenwood.*

Good evening, fans! Tonight I'm going to show you my secret recipe for making really great spaghetti if your dad is away being Elvis. First, fill a saucepan with water. While you're waiting for the water to boil, pour a large jar of extra-chunky spaghetti sauce carefully into another pan—

The phone interrupted my show. I picked it up.

"Josh," a voice said loudly. "This is your dad. I'm in the middle of the dang hotel lobby and my cell battery is shot so I had to use one of the lobby phones. Can you hear me or not?" My dad seemed to be shouting over some mumbling background noise I couldn't identify.

"Yeah, it's okay, go ahead."

His voice kept shouting. "Well, I was in this big rush to get here and had all this crap to remember—the speakers, the mike, the music—and then I got to the hotel and realized what I had completely forgotten."

"What?"

"My daggone costume," he hollered. "They didn't want people to see me before the wedding because I'm supposed to be a surprise, so I didn't come in costume like I usually do," he continued babbling. "I had the costume hanging right beside the front door so I wouldn't forget it, and then what happens? I walk out and leave it behind—jeez." He let out a long frustrated sigh.

I pictured him going onstage in his old jeans, faded T-shirt, and grass-stained sneakers: *Um, howdy folks, forgot my costume tonight, hahaha. Just imagine me as Elvis, okay?*

"Do you have a piece of paper and pencil handy?" my dad continued yelling in my ear.

My spaghetti sauce was splattering all over the top of the stove in little lava-like explosions, but I grabbed a pencil and paper. "Yeah. Okay."

"Here's what I want you to do. I want you to call Viv—"

There was that name again. Viv. The lady I'd meet "eventually," my dad had said. The woman who had called the first night I arrived in Chicago. The potential new girlfriend.

"She's probably working late in her store. Here's how

84

to get in touch with her." He rattled off a phone number. "Just give her a call and ask if she'll come over and pick up the stuff I forgot and bring it to me. Tell her it's a big emergency. Tell her I'll buy her an expensive dinner any-where she wants in Chicago—"

"I'm not telling her that," I interrupted. "Why can't you give her a call?"

"Because I've used up every last cent I've got on this dang pay phone. I had to borrow a dime from the desk clerk just to get through to you, and I've still got to do a sound check and everything else. Don't argue with me, Josh, okay? It's been nothing but a disaster so far tonight. Tell Viv to bring the stuff to the Highland Hotel on Winchester. I'm in Ballroom #2. Got that? Highland. Winchester. Ballroom #2."

I considered telling my dad he could relax because I'd found the perfect job for him. He could go ahead and give up being Elvis that night if he wanted to. But I didn't feel like shouting all of the details into the phone with who knows what happening in the background. Plus, if the wed-ding people had already paid him, he probably couldn't pack up his show and walk out, right? I'd save the news until the next morning as a surprise. *Ta-da,* I'd announce. *I found you a job two doors down from Murphy's. Isn't that great?*

"You're going to call Viv, right?" my dad asked one more time.

"Sure," I answered in a reluctant voice. "What if she isn't there?"

"She'll be there. Trust me," he said, and then hung up.

I was pretty annoyed as I dialed Viv's number. Once again, it was me bailing out my dad. Josh to the rescue.

A girl answered the phone, and I asked if I could speak to Viv.

"Who's calling, please?" the voice said coolly, as if she was Viv's official phone call screener. I didn't really want to give my name, but what choice did I have? After I said, "Josh Greenwood," there was a strange pause.

"Hello?" I repeated, in case the phone had gone dead.

"I'll get her," the voice said quickly.

The woman who came to the phone after that was definitely the same one who had called the first night I arrived in Chicago. "How are things going for you in Chicago, Josh?" she gushed. "Are you settled in yet? How do you like your new school? How's your grandmother doing?" It kind of gave me the creeps that the woman knew so much about me. I gave the shortest answers I could, hoping she would get the hint that I wasn't very interested in blabbing about my life to a complete stranger.

When I finally did manage to get a word in about my dad leaving the house without his Elvis costume, the woman gave an overly long, overly loud laugh. "That's just like Jerry, isn't it? Always forgetting something. Give me about fifteen minutes to finish up my work here at the store, and I'll be right over, hon."

So I was about to meet the mysterious Viv.

Although I didn't know it at the time, I was also going to come face to face with Elvisly Yours.

14. Peace, Love, and Vegetarian Spaghetti

About fifteen minutes later, Viv appeared on my dad's doorstep. She was close to my mom's age, I guessed, but she was a lot shorter and her hair was a fake coppery shade that reminded me of the color of pennies after they have gone through the washing machine a few times. Everything about Viv was shiny, I noticed. Shiny lipstick. Shiny jewelry. Shiny penny-colored hair.

"Josh," she said, reaching out to hug me despite the fact I didn't want to be hugged. A half-dozen shiny bracelets slid down her arms, so there was this jarring, clanging noise in my ears, as if I was being hugged by wind chimes. "I'm Vivian. It's wonderful to finally meet you." She moved to one side and gestured to the tall and skinny girl who was standing on the porch behind her. "This is my daughter, Ivory, but you've probably met her already in school."

The girl behind Viv appeared to have just stepped out of a 1960s time warp. A knitted rainbow beret was perched on her very straight, shoulder-length brown hair. She was wearing a fringed leather vest and jeans with '60s-type patches of daisies, yellow smiley faces, and peace signs sewn all over them. That's what gave me my first clue.

My dad. Viv. Peace signs. Elvisly Yours. . . .

The girl looked over at me and a smile slid slowly across her face. I couldn't tell for sure if she was the one who had sent me the notes, but I swear you could see she was enjoying a private little laugh about something inside her head. "Hey," she said cheerfully, lifting up one arm in a small wave. "How's it going?"

"Would you like to stay here or come with us, Josh?" Viv asked as she took the clothes hanger I'd been holding uncomfortably in one hand since opening the door. I pretended to give this a few seconds of thought before I told her thanks for inviting me but I wanted to hang out at home instead.

Except then, time-warp girl announced she wanted to stay, too. "I'll just wait here with Josh until you get back," she told her mom, as if this was a totally polite thing to do—inviting yourself into somebody else's house without even being asked. And her mom (being a totally polite person, too) said it was fine if her daughter stayed.

"See you." Ivory waved as her mom headed back to the car. Then she brushed past me like one of those fanatics who come to your door with their Bibles, determined to convert you right then and there. Ivory didn't have a Bible in her hand, but she still gave me the same uncomfortable, edgy feeling—as if she was going to convert me to something. I just didn't know what it was.

"Nice house," she said, finding her own way into the living room. Her eyes flickered over everything, taking it all in like she was memorizing it. My dad's living room is pretty worn-out, to be honest. The old tan couch was left over from the years when my mom had lived in the house. It had permanent butt dents in the cushions and round coffee stains on the armrests. We hadn't picked up our Zippy's pizza box from the night before, either, so the whole room smelled like stale pepperoni and cheese.

I stood uncomfortably in the living room doorway, completely clueless about what to say to Ivory. Back in Boston, I was friends with some girls, and they were okay when you were with a group of them, but getting stuck talking to one girl always made me nervous. My neck would start to feel warm and prickly, or I'd get an itch on my scalp. Or worse yet, my eyebrow. *God, I hated that eyebrow thing.* The longer a girl talked to me, the more my eyebrow would feel like some large biting insect had landed on it.

So I definitely didn't want to be stuck hanging around in my dad's empty living room with a girl I didn't even know. I plucked the remote from between the couch cushions. "Here's the clicker," I said, sliding it across the coffee table, "if you want to watch some TV." I was hoping Ivory would get the hint that she was supposed to stay in the living room and entertain herself until her mom came back.

She didn't.

She followed me into the kitchen, where I had left my plate of half-eaten spaghetti sitting on the table when I got up to answer the door. Moving smoothly toward the kitchen window, Ivory pushed aside the curtains to peer outside. "Nice yard."

I watched as Ivory circled the rest of the room, picking up things, silently studying them, and then putting them back down. She nosed around the spices in the spice rack, picked up my dad's guitar-shaped salt and pepper shakers, and shook a tin of gourmet popcorn with a picture of Elvis on the lid. "All shook up," she said with a laugh, as if I would think this was funny. Which I didn't.

In fact, my neck was starting to feel as if it was being attacked by fire ants. "Do you want something to eat— some spaghetti or something?" I asked because I couldn't come up with anything else to keep the girl from examining every detail of our life.

Ivory shook her head. "The label on your jar says meat

sauce." She pointed an accusing finger at the empty glass jar sitting on top of the stove where Chef Josh had left it at the end of his show. "I'm a vegetarian."

Although I didn't really believe meat sauce contained anything other than a few meat-flavored chemicals, I wasn't going to argue with a vegetarian wearing a rainbow beret. I just concentrated on twisting my pasta as neatly as I could onto my fork, as if I was going for the Olympics in spaghetti twisting. Maybe if I stopped talking to the girl completely, she would get the hint. It was a technique that worked with my dad sometimes.

But Ivory seemed oblivious. Pulling up a chair, she sat across from me with her elbows on the table and her chin resting on her hands. She had chipped purple nail polish and a silver ring around her right thumb.

"Does your dad ever say anything about my mom?"

I could feel the red fire ants crawling farther up my neck. *Great. Perfect.* Now I was going to get grilled about my dad's love life by my dad's girlfriend's daughter. (Or whatever she was.)

Note to Dad: In the future, don't date women with daughters my age.

I thought about telling Ivory that my dad dated so *many* women it was hard to keep track of them all—but instead I ended up saying that my dad didn't talk much about his dates. "No matter who it is," I said, shoveling another forkful of spaghetti into my mouth. Ivory was quiet for a while, as if mulling this over.

"So what's your opinion of Listerine?" she asked, changing the subject.

"Listerine?"

"Our school—Charles Lister. We call it Listerine," she said, pulling her feet up onto the chair and wrapping her arms around the front of her legs. "What do you think of it?"

"Oh yeah, Listerine." I forced a laugh, as if I'd already figured out this name myself. Which I hadn't. "It's okay, I guess."

A sneaky look spread across Ivory's face. "And how about my notes? Have you seen the messages I've been leaving on your locker this week?" she asked.

That's when everything finally became clear. The notes weren't coming from some middle school gang planning to torment me for the next four months. They didn't have some sinister, hidden meaning. They had been left by my dad's girlfriend's weird daughter. *Didn't I look like an idiot, right?*

Not wanting to reveal that her peace-sign note had caused me to skip the bus and walk two miles home that afternoon, I told Ivory I didn't really like notes and stuff on my locker. In general.

"No?" Ivory picked up an apple from the bowl of fruit

on our table and rubbed it on the corner of her shirt before taking a large, loud bite. "I thought they'd make you feel like you had some friends at Listerine."

Note to Ivory: Friends sign notes. They don't leave demented smiley faces and bizarre messages.

"School's fine." I could feel my shoulders tensing up as I tried to get Ivory to understand what I was saying. "And I'd rather not have everybody knowing about my dad being Elvis, so you don't need to keep leaving notes on my locker and writing things like 'Elvisly Yours.' Everything's good at school." I hoped this sounded convincing.

"What's wrong with people knowing about your dad?" Ivory studied me. Her eyes were dark brown and had an unsettling way of staring at your face for too long without blinking. "I think it's really cool."

"I don't want people talking about it, that's all." I could tell my voice was getting a nervous edge to it and my shoulders were moving even closer to my ears.

"You must be a Leo," Ivory said, taking another loud apple bite. "That's why."

"A Leo?"

"Your sign—you know, Scorpio, Libra, Aries. When's your birthday?"

"The beginning of August."

Ivory gave a knowing smile. "That explains it."

"What explains what?"

"Why you're like you are about your dad." Ivory pointed a purple fingernail in my direction. "You're a Leo. That's why. You worry too much about what other people think of you. That's a Leo."

I wanted to say there was no way that somebody who had met me for the first time about a half hour earlier (and who had watched me eat a plate of spaghetti and that was about it) could know what I was like. And I also didn't believe a bunch of stars could tell much about me, either. But Ivory had already moved on.

She reached for the morning newspaper, which was still sitting on the table, and asked if it was okay if she did the crossword puzzle. "If nobody's done it yet," she said, digging through her purse, looking for something to write with.

"Sure, go ahead," I said, secretly hoping it was the kind of thing that would keep her busy until her mom got back. A few clues like *ACROSS: Edible Asian squid. DOWN: Small river in Mozambique* would be helpful. I headed into the living room to watch some television and, fortunately, Ivory didn't follow me.

About an hour later, Viv returned. "Well, I got to the hotel just in time," she announced loudly as she stepped into my dad's house. Even though it was dark, a pair of sunglasses was still perched on her copper hair. Plucking the glasses from the top of her head and shoving them into her purse, she said, "I got your dad's outfit to the dressing room right before everything was supposed to start. You should've seen how the place was set up, Josh. It was a big wedding. Expensive." She drew out the word to emphasize it. "But Jerry had the crowd in the palm of his hand. One of the hotel staff let me peek through the door for his opening song. I told them I was Elvis's girlfriend." That long laugh again. "He sang 'Blue Suede Shoes' first. Have you seen him do that one?"

I thought about answering, *no, but the Summerland Mall probably did.*

"Well, the stage is dark, and then Jerry comes out. He starts singing slowly at first, but when he gets to the 'blue suede shoes' part, he begins dancing like Elvis. He gets down on one knee at one part and moves to the music and strums a guitar—really, you wouldn't believe it." She shook her head. "I was just amazed at how good he was, standing up there onstage all by himself, acting and singing in front of all those people like he wasn't even nervous."

Note to Viv: You can stop talking anytime now.

"He's getting better and better, don't you think so?" Viv looked at me as if she expected me to agree, although in my mind there was no difference between my dad being a good Elvis or a bad Elvis. The problem was "being Elvis" in the first place. So all I said was that he practiced a lot.

"Where's Ivory?" Viv glanced into the living room, where the TV was still blaring with nobody in front of it.

"The kitchen." I pointed. "She's working on a cross-word."

Then Ivory magically appeared behind us in the hall-way. She glided innocently out of the kitchen as if she hadn't been standing there taking notes about every single word that had been said.

"Did you and Josh enjoy talking and catching up on school?" Viv asked.

Note to parents: What do you expect us to answer—*no, we hated each other? Please don't ever put us in the same room again?*

Ivory cast a polite smile in my direction. "Sure," she said.

At that point, I would have predicted there was zero possibility of a friendship developing between the two of us, despite what our parents might have hoped. Ivory and I were complete opposites, that was pretty clear. And with her knitted beret and hippie outfit, she was dangerously close to being the kind of freak I stayed away from like the plague.

But Ivory didn't see it that way, I guess.

As she and her mom walked to their car, Ivory glanced back at the screen door, where I was waiting to turn off the porch light once they reached the driveway. It was a warm and muggy night. Clouds of gnats swarmed around the door, but even with the bugs and the dim pool of yellow light, I could still see what Ivory did when she turned. She lifted two fingers, grinned, and flashed me a peace sign in the darkness. Ivory, it seemed, was not going to give up easily.

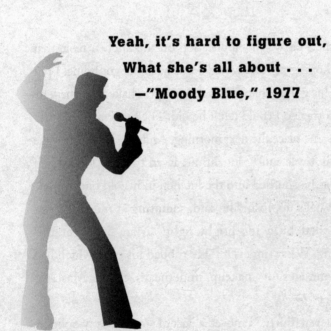

Yeah, it's hard to figure out,
What she's all about . . .
—"Moody Blue," 1977

15. Solitaire

I left the Harpy's job application on the kitchen table that night, hoping my dad would see it when he got home. I put one of his guitar-shaped salt and pepper shakers on the left-hand corner so I could tell if he did. The salt shaker was still in the same place the next morning. And my dad didn't wake up until it was almost lunchtime. Even then, he looked half asleep as he shuffled into the kitchen in his old blue robe.

"What's up, Josh?" he said, squinting at me as if I was surrounded by a too-bright light. "Man, I'm beat this morning. What time is it?" He rubbed his eyes, which had dark smudges of makeup underneath them. Mascara? Eyeliner? *Jeesh.*

"Eleven-thirty." I moved a jack of spades in my Solitaire game. It was my fifth game of the morning, and I hadn't won a single one yet.

"God, is it really that late?" my dad croaked hoarsely,

glancing toward the kitchen window. "Where did the morning go?" He moved over to the counter to start the coffeemaker. I watched him scoop the coffee carelessly into the machine like he did every morning. Grains scattered across the counter. "So," he said, sweeping up the mess with the side of his hand and dumping it back in the canister. "What did you think of Viv?"

"She was okay." I tried not to sound very convinced.

My dad shook his head. "I'll tell you what, she saved my butt last night. I don't know what I would've done if she hadn't brought that stuff over. I've got to get my act together and be more organized like your mother, right?" he said, coming over to the table with his coffee and a big box of Cheerios tucked under his arm. "Viv's pretty different from your mom, isn't she?"

I could feel my defend-my-mom side starting to come out. "What do you mean?"

"Just how she dresses and acts—kind of a nontraditional person, I guess," he said, sitting down. I slid my cards over to give him more space.

"Mom's like that sometimes," I insisted, although right then I couldn't come up with any examples that would qualify as nontraditional except for the fact that my mom had season tickets to the summer theater in Boston and once took a pottery class. She also wore flowery-type scarves sometimes.

"Viv owns a vintage clothing store in town," my dad said through a mouthful of Cheerios. "It's called Viv's Vintage. She sells all kinds of old clothing. Not old like worn-out, but old as in antiques—you know, stuff from the past."

Clearly, Ivory did most of her shopping there.

"So what did you think of her daughter?" my dad continued. "Viv said Ivory came along so she could meet you."

I could feel my face redden as I told my dad she was nice but not really my kind of person. Hoping he would just drop the topic altogether, I pretended to concentrate on how to move a five of diamonds to another spot in my game. But my dad took a long swallow of coffee and said, "Maybe you could hang out with her at school or go to the movies with her or something like that. Just to be nice."

"Dad—" I gave him a disgusted look. "Just stop it."

I think he got the message. Changing the subject, he began describing how great the show had gone after his costume had arrived. How the bride and groom were completely surprised.

Note to Dad: I'll bet they were.

"They thought they were just getting a little video show with photographs from their families and childhood and that kind of stuff. They didn't know their friends had hired the King to perform!" my dad said, switching to his Elvis voice. "You shoulda seen the bride's face when I walked over to her table and sang 'Can't Help Falling in Love' at the end of the set. Man, I didn't even screw up the line about how the river flows surely to the sea. I always forget 'surely,' but this time"—he snapped his fingers—"perfect."

Before he started performing the whole song for me, I figured I would point out the Harpy's application, which was still sitting on the table. Tugging it out from underneath the salt shaker, I explained how I had seen a great job on my way home from school. "I got off at the wrong stop," I lied, not wanting to reveal the whole story of the Post-it notes on my locker, "and I was walking past Harpy's when I saw the sign about needing help in the store. The guy told me they could probably hire you this weekend if you wanted."

Dad spent about five seconds skimming the top page and didn't even turn to the second one, which was the application itself. "Thanks, Josh," he said, sliding it back across the table, "but I'm having way too much fun with what I'm doing now." Breaking into a smile, he leaned back in his chair and crossed his arms. "You know what some old guy told me last night? That I sounded exactly like Elvis. He said if he closed his eyes, he couldn't tell the difference."

I wanted to shout at my dad: *Don't you get it? I found you a job. A real job. With benefits (whatever that meant). They said they could hire you tomorrow. At least you could give it a little thought instead of going on and on about how much you sound like some old guy's idea of Elvis.*

Sitting there, I had the strange feeling that my mom had probably been in this same chair once, looking at the same blue-checkered kitchen wallpaper, feeling the same frustration at my dad. I'd heard stories from my mom about how little money they'd had when they were first married. Nobody could break a leg or hit a tree, Mom told me, because they had no cash to fix anything. Sometimes, we still used that saying with each other. "Don't break a leg or hit a tree," we'd joke whenever either one of us was going out somewhere.

I made one last attempt to convince my dad. "Couldn't you just go in and talk to Harpy and find out what the job is?"

Dad set his coffee cup on the table and stood up, stretching out his back. "Thanks for thinking of me, Josh, but things are going okay with my Elvis shows. I'm making pretty good money and business is picking up a little each week. The more people hear about me, the more gigs I'll get." He smiled confidently. "You've got to take chances in this life, Josh. You'll see. If you want to do what you love, you've got to take chances."

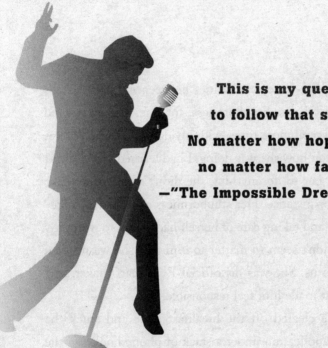

This is my quest,
to follow that star,
No matter how hopeless,
no matter how far . . .
—"The Impossible Dream," 1972

16. Winning and Losing

There were a lot of similarities between my dad and his neighbor Gladys. Stubbornness, for one. Having visited Gladys several more times with my dad to pick up scarves or check on how she was doing, I had learned you couldn't convince her to do anything she didn't want to do. Like eating, for instance. Her stubbornness about eating regular meals and taking care of herself had begun to worry my dad. It didn't seem to matter to him that she wasn't even related to us. She was his official Elvis scarf maker, so I guess that made him feel responsible.

As he cleared off the breakfast table and stuck the Harpy's application under a stack of phone books on the counter, he asked me if I'd stop by and visit Gladys that afternoon. "Maybe you can convince her to eat something for lunch today, because I haven't been having much luck," he said as he stacked the dishes on the counter.

"Yesterday when I stopped by, she hadn't eaten a thing all day."

Needless to say, I wasn't too excited about the prospect of spending part of my Saturday encouraging an old lady to eat lunch. I'd just spent the whole morning playing Solitaire waiting for my dad to wake up. And now he wanted me to go and visit the neighbors. On the other hand, it was a way to get out of the house so I wouldn't have to hear more details about his Elvis show, along with little reenactments of various parts, which he would bring up at random throughout the day. *Hey, Josh, forgot to tell you about this. . . .*

Gladys or Elvis, it was a tough choice.

I chose Gladys.

When I knocked on her door a while later, she seemed pleased to see me. "I was hoping someone would come by and pay this old lady a visit today," Gladys said brightly. She was dressed in a lime-green jogging suit instead of her bathrobe, which I took as a good sign, and her hair didn't look as much like couch stuffing. Another good sign. "Come on in," she said, holding the door open. "Tell me your name again. I know you're a friend of Elvis, I just can't remember who you are. I'm eighty-seven, you know."

"Josh."

"That's right." She shook her head back and forth. "Let me tell you, Josh, it's hell being old."

Without even stopping, I said, "It's hell being thirteen."

Gladys thought this was very funny (which my mom wouldn't have). She patted my arm and gave one of her creaky laughs. "I'll trade with you anytime, my dear," she said over her shoulder as she shuffled down the hall. "You take eighty-seven. I'll take thirteen."

Which makes you think. It really does.

When we got to the kitchen, Gladys poked around as if she was looking for something edible to offer me. "Are you hungry? Would you like a snack or something?" she said, opening the refrigerator. From where I was standing, I could see it was pretty empty—just a jug of milk, a bag of apples, and a loaf of bread. The rest of the place hadn't changed much, either: same piles of newspapers and junk mail scattered across the table and counters.

"My dad said you needed some help with lunch," I mumbled.

Gladys closed the refrigerator door and made her way along the counter, holding one edge with her hand. "Oh, I don't eat lunch anymore. No appetite for it," she said, sitting down carefully at the kitchen table and closing her eyes as if to show there was no point in arguing with her about it. "Costs too much."

My grandma and her friends were the same way about money. They liked to go to the free seniors' lunch offered every Wednesday and Sunday at the Shadyside Episcopal Church. I'd gone with them once or twice, although it was kind of embarrassing to watch how they would sneak extra packets of jam into their purses and then trade each other for different ones on the bus ride back. "I'll give you three raspberry jams for one honey," they'd say, passing the little packets back and forth. On Fridays, her group usually went to the $4.99 All-You-Can-Eat lunch buffet at the Seafood Palace. As far as I know, they didn't steal anything from there.

"Do you have any friends who go out for lunch?" I asked, not even sure if Chicago had lunch buffets for senior citizens. Or if Gladys had any friends.

Gladys shook her head stubbornly. "I'm not hungry, but thank you for asking."

I suggested soup, cheese sandwiches, salad, and even a pepperoni pizza. But Gladys kept insisting she wasn't hungry. A bit. That's what she kept saying. Not a bit.

"How about something sweet like . . ." I searched for something to suggest. My grandma had a sweet tooth and my mom often complained about how many desserts she ate. "You've got to watch your sugar, Mom," she'd say impatiently, but it didn't seem to help because there was usually a half-empty box of chocolates on her kitchen table whenever we came to visit. She was a big fan of donuts, too. Those glazed cinnamon ones from the grocery store. Three packs for $1.99.

"How about a donut or something?" It was my last desperate idea.

Gladys seemed to think about this for a minute. I was holding my breath and waiting for her to insist (yet again) that she wasn't hungry, but instead a smile slowly creased across her tissue-paper skin. "You know, a donut might taste good. I haven't had one in such a long time I don't even remember what they taste like."

There was a little donut shop called Dino's around the corner. Dad and I often stopped there on Sunday mornings to pick up a few of their frosted twists. We'd eat them in the car and get flecks of sugar glaze all over our clothes.

I told Gladys I would buy a box of donuts for us. "Oh, you needn't go to all that bother," she insisted, but I said it was no problem. I could walk there. "Well, take some money at least." She pushed a crumpled ten-dollar bill into my hand and I headed out the door, hoping Dino's Donuts would still be open.

When I got there, the red-faced woman who was running the counter went through the choices in one long, bored list: "Raspberrychocolatestrawberryvanillalemonspice." Since I had no clue what kind of fillings Gladys would like, I told the lady to give me one of each.

"That'll be three-fifty." She plunked the donuts in a box and pushed it toward me with an annoyed sigh, as if daring me to ask for something else—which I didn't. I also didn't tell her that she had a large blob of chocolate frosting on the front of her Dino's shirt.

After I got back, Gladys spent the next ten minutes picking out the ones she wanted. "I think maybe I'll try that lemon one. I do like lemon meringue pie . . . no, strawberry's my favorite . . . on second thought, that spice one looks good. . . ."

I couldn't believe it when she ended up finishing two and a half donuts by herself. She ate them as if they were pieces of pie—first dividing them into neat triangles and then picking up each bite with her fork. When she was done, she scraped every bit of leftover jelly off her plate too. My mom would have had a fit at the fact we ate nothing except a box of donuts for lunch. But it didn't kill us, right?

Afterward, I suggested playing a game of cards and Gladys found an old rubber-banded deck in one of her kitchen drawers. I tried teaching her some of the games my grandma and I usually played, but Gladys seemed to have trouble remembering anything with a lot of rules (or maybe it was all the sugar we ate). "Oh, now that's too complicated," she'd say, flapping her hands at me. "Teach me something simpler." So I ended up showing her the little kids' version of Go Fish—where you just need to find matches for your cards.

After winning two rounds, I tried hard to let Gladys

win. Sometimes I wouldn't lay down a matching pair if I had one, or I'd draw extra cards from the pile so there would be more in my hand. "Don't you have a match?" I kept asking, trying to encourage her. It takes a lot of thought and strategy to lose, I found out. Way more than it takes to win.

This was a lesson I would remember much later on.

But finally, Gladys won a round. You should have seen the look on her face. She waved her empty hands in the air. "Look at that. Look at that. No cards! I'm the winning fisherman—fisherwoman," she shouted proudly.

I had to admit I felt good about making her happy. Like there was this golden halo around my head all of a sudden and wings sprouting from my back. *Good angel Josh.* Could guys be angels? Okay, just nice divorced kid Josh. Maybe something like that could go on a gold plaque under my face: JOSH GREENWOOD—GOOD FRIEND, SOCCER PLAYER, DIVORCED KID, AND NICE TO OLD LADIES.

When I finally left Gladys's house after finishing three games of Go Fish and splitting one more donut with her, she gave me an armful of scarves to take back to my dad. "Give these to Elvis whenever you see him," she said. "And you let me know if he needs more and I'll get busy making them."

As I headed back to my dad's place with the scarf rainbow tucked under my arm and a stomach full of donut grease, I felt like things in Chicago were looking up.

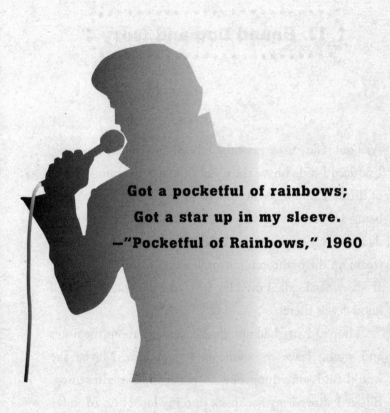

Got a pocketful of rainbows;
Got a star up in my sleeve.
—"Pocketful of Rainbows," 1960

17. Hound Dog and Ivory

As I got ready for school the following Monday morning, I noticed I didn't have the usual stomach-churning feeling of dread. I no longer needed to worry about bizarre notes being left on my locker—or kids finding out about my dad—which was a major relief. Rubbing a circle in the steam on the bathroom mirror, I actually smiled at myself. It was what I called my Hey Josh smile, just to let myself know I was there.

I hoped Ivory had gotten the message about the notes and would leave me alone at school now. Maybe she would find something new to befriend, like a lost dog. But as I shoved my backpack into my locker on Monday morning, a voice said, "Did the rest of your dad's show go okay?" Ivory stood directly behind me, holding an armful of books. This time, she wasn't wearing the hippie outfit with the ridiculous rainbow beret; instead, an orange-and-brown fringed poncho floated around her shoulders. To be honest, she looked like an unraveling carpet.

I glanced around to see who was within listening range. A guy from my math class was just opening his locker, four doors down from mine. Two earbuds were stuck in his ears and his head bobbed up and down to the music. Until he turned off the sound, I was probably safe. "Yes, fine," I answered over my left shoulder, trying to sound impatient. I crammed my World History textbook into my locker, crumpling a few of the pages.

"Mom said he sounded really good. What she heard, that is."

Note to Ivory: I know what your mom said. I was there, remember?

I wondered if she was doing this on purpose. *Let's see how many ways I can talk about your dad being Elvis without mentioning his name?*

"I've gotta get to English class. The teacher is giving a quiz this morning," I replied, slamming my locker shut. I figured this would give the girl a clue. *Locker slam equals conversation ending.*

But she didn't get the hint.

"I'm going that way, too. I've got World History next—what fun." She rolled her eyes.

Note to self: Next time you run into Ivory, ask where

she is going first, then tell her you have to go the opposite direction. Even if you don't.

As we headed down the hall, I could tell people were noticing that I was walking beside a girl who looked like an unraveling brown carpet and they were probably drawing at least one of the following conclusions: (a) We were friends. (b) I was somebody who liked to hang out with strange people. (c) If I liked to hang out with strange people, I was somebody who should be avoided.

Looking for a way out, I decided to use the guys' restroom as my excuse, although if you go in there just to check out how your hair looks or wash your hands, trust me, you get really weird looks. But I was desperate.

"Hey," I said, nodding in the direction of the approaching sign. "I'll, uh—" I stumbled over my words. "I'll, uh, catch up with you later, okay?" Then I headed through the guys' door and tried to look as if I had accidentally touched a really disgusting doorknob as I scrubbed my hands at the sink.

Fortunately, Ivory didn't locate me again until lunchtime. I was eating at the end of a table when she strolled past with her tray. I had the feeling this was not exactly a coincidence. Out of all of the rows crisscrossing the cafeteria, she just happened to pick mine to pass through, right?

"Josh," she said, turning back to look at me with a fake surprised expression on her face. "Are you sitting here all by yourself?" Her eyes roamed slowly down the length of the table.

I was not sitting by myself in the literal sense of the word. In fact, there were six or seven guys at my table. I just didn't happen to be sitting next to them. "I always sit here," I said, feeling my shoulders beginning to tense up. "It's fine."

Ivory's eyes glanced back at the table. I could tell that she was noting the four empty seats between me and the rest of the group. While she was standing there, the guy I'd seen on the first day—the one with the studded dog collar—passed by. He was carrying a cafeteria tray, which held an enormous pile of French fries. Mount Everest in fries. "Digger," Ivory called out. "Come over here and meet my friend Josh."

Please no, keep going, Digger.

But apparently Digger had pin-drop hearing (or the whole thing had been staged beforehand) because he turned around and came back to meet me. I could feel the warmth creeping up my neck as he stood next to Ivory. I didn't even need to turn my head to know the guys at my table were all watching the scene silently.

Note to self: Cross this table off tomorrow's seating list.

Ivory introduced me as her friend from Boston. "My mom knows his dad," she explained, giving me a smirky

117

smile. "And this is Digger," she said, playfully leaning her head on the dog-collar guy's shoulder. "His real name is Paul Diggs, but he usually goes by Digger."

Up close, the guy looked like a high schooler. He was big (overweight big) and his fleshy face was seriously broken out. "Nice to meet you," he said in a mumbling voice, without looking up. My eyes just couldn't keep from staring at the dog collar. It was red with silver pointed studs. Was it a real dog collar or not? And why would you choose to wear a real dog collar around your neck? Did he wear it all day? Even at home around his parents? Even to bed at night?

"Why don't you come and sit with us?" Ivory continued, in a friendly voice, as if we were having a perfectly normal conversation. She nodded toward the far side of the cafeteria. "We always sit over there. There's plenty of space and we could introduce you to our group, right, Digger?"

Of course, the tables she meant were the ones I'd seen on the first day. The place where the losers sat, where food thrown in the direction of the garbage cans sometimes landed: crumpled milk cartons and torn packets of ketchup and who knows what else. *Great.* An entire school full of kids and my dad's girlfriend's daughter had to be one of the garbage can people. Not only that, she was standing in the middle of the cafeteria, where anybody could hear her, and inviting me to be one, too.

That's when I began to wonder if, somewhere between Boston and Chicago, things had changed for me. I still felt like I was the same person—the same funny Josh who hung out with the popular group at my old school and who was friends with Brian and the other guys—but if I was being singled out by people like Ivory and Digger in Chicago, maybe I wasn't the person I thought I was. Nobody else seemed very anxious to invite me into their group of friends, did they? Had I somehow become a loser magnet overnight?

"Thanks, I'm fine here," I mumbled to Ivory, keeping my head down.

Ivory shrugged. "No problem."

I didn't even watch as she and the dog-collar guy walked away. Instead, I kept looking over my shoulder, pretending I was more interested in what was going on behind me. When a few of the guys at the table glanced in my direction, I shook my head and gave the wide-eyed "what the heck was that" look, trying to communicate the message, without saying it in words, that I had no clue why those two weird people had stopped by the table to talk to me. They certainly weren't my friends. Which was true, I hoped.

**You ain't never caught a rabbit
and you ain't no friend of mine.**
—"Hound Dog," 1956

18. Viv's Vintage

For the rest of the week, Ivory managed to run into me at school at least once a day, although it was never at the same time or the same place. I think she planned it that way so I couldn't avoid her. If I never knew exactly when she would tap me on the shoulder or call out hello across the hall, I couldn't take a different route. Even when I did, she somehow managed to find me.

I still couldn't decide on her motives, either: whether Ivory thought she was just being nice to me because her mom was dating my dad (or whatever they were doing), or if she knew she was humiliating me and enjoyed seeing how far she could take it.

To make matters worse, my dad had started spending more and more time with her mom. Often when I got home from school, I found a note left on the kitchen table—AT VIV'S STORE or GONE OUT SHOPPING WITH VIV.

I also couldn't help noticing that my dad had stuck a photo of Viv on the refrigerator, right in the middle of his haphazard collection of postcards, vacation magnets, and pictures of me as a drooling preschooler. The photo showed the two of them smiling together in some dark restaurant booth—although Viv had red-eye and looked slightly possessed in the picture, which I thought was funny.

When my dad started talking about a business workshop he wanted to go to with Viv, I should have known I was in trouble. We were sitting around waiting for a movie to start one night when he said, "There's this marketing workshop next weekend that Viv and I would like to take, and we were hoping maybe you and Ivory could watch the store for a few hours while we're gone."

"What?" I stared at my dad.

He reached for a bag of chips on the coffee table and shoved a handful in his mouth. Crumbs scattered across his shirt. "It's just for one Saturday, and I told Viv you're very responsible and good with numbers, so you could work the register and Ivory could help the customers. The guy who runs the barbershop next door will be around all day if there are any problems."

Since I couldn't exactly say Ivory was one of the last people on earth I wanted to spend an entire Saturday with, I told my dad I already had other plans. School stuff. Lots of school stuff. "Couldn't you get somebody else?"

My dad gave me his best salesman look. "This is important to me, Josh. I need to learn how to do Web sites and press releases and stuff like that for my Elvis business. I'm just asking you to give Ivory a hand for a few hours in Viv's store."

Note to Dad: An entire Saturday is not a few hours.

"The rest of the weekend is yours," he said, brushing off his shirt. "I don't ask you for help that often, do I?" *There was the guilt line designed especially to plunge straight into my thirteen-year-old heart.*

"Sure, whatever," I said in a frustrated voice. Getting up, I pretended to storm out, leaving him to watch his stupid movie and eat his bag of chips by himself.

Clearly, my movie boycott didn't work, because a week later, at nine o'clock in the morning, we were in the car heading to Viv's store. Dad looked remarkably un-Elvis for once. He had trimmed his sideburns shorter than usual and he wore a plain white business shirt and blue pants that I seemed to remember were part of his Murphy's days.

"Haven't been to a class in years," he said nervously as we drove.

Viv's store was in a small strip of tired-looking stores and businesses not far from Murphy's Shoes. A sign above the place spelled out VIV'S VINTAGE in faded purple letters, with a daisy (what else, right?) used in place of the apostrophe. Crammed with junk, the front window looked like a bizarre prop collection for a Hollywood movie. There were mannequins in sequined dresses, a white claw-foot bathtub full of old hats, large Japanese fans, and even, in one corner, a plaster head of Elvis with part of his nose chipped off.

My dad pointed at the Elvis head as we walked past. "Isn't that great? Viv says she's going to loan it to me one of these days. Maybe I'll put it in one of my upstairs windows and get the neighbors talking," he joked.

Note to Dad: I'm sure they already are.

Viv was standing at the door when we got there and a string of metal bells jangled as we walked in. She hadn't turned on the lights yet, so the store was still dark and smelled faintly of mothballs. It reminded me of visiting my grandma's house in Florida. I always stayed in her spare bedroom, and whenever I opened the bedroom's narrow closet to put my suitcases inside, that was the smell that came wafting out. An old but friendly smell.

Reaching out, Viv squeezed my shoulders. "Thank you for giving up your Saturday to help us out. That was so kind of you, Josh." The way she said it, gushing over every word, made me suspect my dad had already told her I wasn't crazy about helping out in the first place.

"Ivory's in the back." Viv pointed toward a bead curtain separating the store from an office. "I'll give you the tour and then we'll be on our way."

The tour was fairly simple since the place only had three rooms—the store, the cramped office behind the bead curtain, and a small closet with a purple door that had the words TRYOUTS HERE painted on it (meaning this was where people could try on the old, mothball-smelling clothes).

Viv showed me how to run the register and how to use the credit card machine. It wasn't as hard as I thought it would be. Just zip the plastic through the slot and punch in a few numbers. No big deal. Ivory came out and sat at the counter, pretending to read a book while we talked. She was wearing a ridiculous black-and-white-striped hat that shaded most of her face. *Think zebra.*

"Well, that's about it," Viv said finally, pulling a purse over her shoulder and jangling her car keys. "You two have fun today and sell a lot of stuff, okay?"

Looking around the store, I didn't believe either one of those things would be possible: fun or sales. In my pocket, I'd brought along a deck of cards and planned to set a new world record by playing Solitaire for the next eight hours straight, with a few breaks in between to eat the lunch and snacks I'd packed.

However, Ivory had other plans and they seemed to include endlessly talking to me. My dad and Viv hadn't even been gone ten minutes when she began telling me every detail of the wonderful book she was reading. Even though I tried to make it pretty clear that I never read stories about dragons and mystical kingdoms and things like that, she still insisted I had to borrow the book someday. "It'll change your life," she said, confidently snapping the cover closed. "I promise."

I didn't like reading in general. I'd been one of the last kids in my first-grade class who learned to read. The experience was something I still tried to avoid thinking about—not only how slowly I used to read, but how embarrassing it had been to sit in the hallway with my "special" tutor trying to sound out words on giant flash cards—

Attempting to change the subject, I asked Ivory how she got her name, since it wasn't exactly what you would call typical.

She explained that it came from a lady who used to work part-time at Viv's Vintage. "Back when my mom was pregnant with me," she said, "this retired lady used to help out in the store on the weekends. There was an old piano in the front window back then, and she and my mom would goof around sometimes and play little songs on it, if the store was quiet. One day, I started kicking right in the middle of 'Chopsticks' and the lady told my mom maybe she should call me Ivory when I was born. So she did."

I know my face must have looked completely blank, because Ivory tapped her fingers on the counter like an imaginary keyboard. "Ivories . . . the name for the keys on the piano. Get it?"

Note to Mom: Thank you for not naming me after any musical instrument. Imagine going through life called Oboe or Cello. Or worse, Tuba.

"How'd you get your name?" Ivory asked, propping her feet up on the counter and tilting her head back to peer at me from underneath the zebra.

I told her my mom wanted a name that didn't rhyme with anything. Of course, then Ivory had to go through all of the words that rhymed with Josh. "What about posh, gosh, wash"—she counted them on her fingers—"slosh, hogwash . . ."

Ignoring my unamused look, Ivory continued rambling on, smoothly slipping in another one of her relationship questions after she had run out of words that rhymed with Josh. "So do you remember anything from when your parents got divorced?" she asked me while unwrapping a piece of gum.

I don't know what made me tell her about the plants, since I hardly ever talked about my parents' divorce with people. Mom and Dad had split up when I was five, so it was hard to remember much about it anyway. But for some reason, I started explaining to Ivory how, after the divorce, my mom had decided to move back to Boston, where she was from. All of our stuff was packed inside a big moving truck. Everything except for the plants, that is.

My mom is a big plant lover—ferns, ivy, tropical plants, that kind of thing—and she decided it would be safer to keep her plants in the backseat of our car rather than the moving truck. "I guess that's when I finally realized that something was seriously wrong—that we were not coming back," I said to Ivory.

I could still remember crying and blubbering over and over, "Why are we taking the plants?" as we drove away from my dad's house one January afternoon with the snow falling around our car like a sad divorce snow globe. Never mind that we were following a big truck with half the house packed inside. It was the stupid plants that bothered me. In my mind, I could still picture those plants filling the entire left side of the car like man-eating Amazon jungle vines: *Josh Greenwood and the Attack of the Divorced Houseplants.*

According to my mom, I threw such a fit about the plants that she finally stopped at a service plaza in Ohio and left the pots sitting on the curb. She often jokes about going back to look for them.

"So that's about all I remember about my parents'

divorce—the plants," I finished quickly, embarrassed at how much I'd said. "I was only five."

Ivory nodded. "I can totally see that." The situation with her dad was different, she explained, because her parents split up when she was a baby and her dad was "out of the picture," in her words. She waved her hand. "No problem, his loss."

The entire time we talked, nobody came into the store. By lunchtime, the jangling doorbells still hadn't made a peep, and I had listened to enough *Phantom of the Opera* on the store speakers to last for about ten lifetimes. When I mentioned how few customers we'd had (like zero), Ivory threw an irritated look in my direction. "It's just a slow time of day. People sleep in on Saturday mornings. What do you expect?"

We did have two customers after lunch. A mom and her screechy-voiced daughter came inside to dig through the hat bathtub. By the time they were finished, it looked like an explosion in the window display. But Ivory convinced them to buy four hats before they left. "It's our Saturday afternoon shoppers' special," she said, turning on the charm. "Buy three and you get one free."

Those hats would end up being our only sales for the day: a grand total of $22.91. Ivory claimed that sales usually picked up in a week or so, once October arrived and people started looking for Halloween costumes.

"Let's see what the zodiac book says business will be like next week." Ivory reached under the counter to pull out a dog-eared book called *365 Days of Personal Horoscopes and Business Forecasts*. It was the kind of paperback you'd find for sale in drugstores next to the magazines or the breath mints. "You would be amazed at how often the predictions in here are right," she told me as she licked her index finger and began searching for the page she wanted.

Laying out a row of cards, I didn't bother to answer.

"According to the book, we're going to see increasing sales next week, with some unpredictability toward the end of the week," Ivory said, looking up from a page.

Right. The hat bathtub will probably sell out.

"I'm supposed to have more opportunities for creativity next week. And you"—she turned to another page—"are supposed to watch out for an unexpected surprise at the beginning of the week."

"Does it say what the surprise is going to be?" I asked, knowing of course that it wouldn't, because that's the way horoscopes are written. To be vague on purpose. So if you found a dollar bill on the sidewalk, you might think that was the unexpected surprise. Or if an airplane crashlanded on your house, that would count, too.

"It just says watch out for an unexpected surprise."

"Oh, okay. Thanks for warning me."

Anybody but Ivory would have picked up on the sarcasm.

But Ivory just continued on in her own little zodiac world. "As a Leo, you need to watch being too impatient this week, too. And your ego can get in the way, if you're not careful." She looked up and caught my annoyed expression. "I'm just reading this for your own good, you know," she insisted, arching her eyebrows.

I wondered what gave Ivory the idea that I needed to know any of this stuff for my own good. Why is it that certain people feel like it's their job to point out what other people need? *Look at yourself in the mirror,* I wanted to say to Ivory. *You wear zebra hats, hang out with guys who wear dog collars, and believe in the stars and planets running your life. I'm not the one with the problems here.*

Checking my watch for the tenth or eleventh time, I decided the hands had definitely stopped. It was only three-thirty and Viv's Vintage stayed open until five-thirty for all of those last-minute shoppers who needed a pair of plaid pants or a nice powder-blue polyester suit. It was going to be a long afternoon.

19. Signs of the Zodiac

As it turned out, Ivory's prediction did come true two days later—which is exactly how horoscopes can pull you into believing in them. After you hear one, you can't keep the little zodiac voice in the back of your mind from whispering maybe the moon and stars do know all.

On Monday morning, the gym teacher took us outside to play baseball. Puddles of water from the downpour we'd had on Sunday still dotted the clay of the ball diamond, but the sky was totally clear and blue. The trees on the far edges of the school property were beginning to change color and the warm air smelled like fall. It made me feel kind of homesick for Boston and my friends.

We lined up on the grass to pick teams. I was picked fourth by a guy named Dave, who looked like he was probably part of the vending machine crowd. First, because he appointed himself the team captain and nobody disagreed, and second, because he wore a sports jersey with his last name plastered across the back.

Fourth wasn't a bad spot to be, I decided. It was better than being picked last—or after a girl. Or a fat guy. Digger, the dog-collar guy, was in the class and he was picked last for the other team. In fact, he wasn't even really picked—the teacher just divided up the last few people with a "you here" and "you over there" arm move. Since nobody knew me that well yet and we hadn't played baseball before, being picked fourth wasn't too bad. Maybe I looked like I had potential.

In the second inning, with our team losing by one run and with two people on base, I went up to the plate. Behind me, I could hear the team captain and a few of the other guys call out, "Go on, Boston dude, hit one out of here." I shaded my eyes against the sun and looked out at the field, which was pretty pathetic. The pitcher for the other team was good, but the outfield was dotted with their last picks, including Digger, who was standing in the farthest part of the field among the tall wet grass and fuzzy weeds. If I could smack one that distance, I was all set.

The ball came sailing toward me, like a fat and juicy grapefruit curving through the air. I swung hard. The crack of the ball meeting my bat sounded like a soda can exploding.

Note to pitcher: In Boston, I'm a very good hitter.

The ball flew toward the outfield, and Digger was just about the only person who had any chance at it, and not much chance at that. I watched him stretch upward so that sky and glove were connected for a brief minute, and then in one slow-motion frame it all began falling apart. Digger started tipping backward, landing heavily on his butt in the grass, and the ball sailed easily into the outfield. My team went nuts, clapping for me and laughing at Digger, who was just getting up and brushing off his wet, grass-covered gym shorts. Home run.

As I jogged around the bases, I could barely keep a big smile from cracking across my face. When you run the bases, it's better to look as if it isn't a big deal, as if this is something you do every day. People take you more seriously that way. So I kept my lips pressed together and my eyes focused on the brown dirt gliding under my feet.

Score one for Ivory's horoscopes.

And then, a few hours later, another unexpected surprise followed the first one. I was reaching for some ketchup and napkins on the condiments table when somebody called out, "Hey, Boston dude." I turned around slowly, half expecting some object to come flying toward my face, because the entire cafeteria experience at Listerine still made me jumpy. But instead, I saw the team captain from gym class strolling over with his tray. *Dave, right?* I tried to reach back in my memory for the name. I was almost positive it was Dave.

"Good hit," he said.

"Yeah, thanks." I put on my home-run straight face again and glanced down at my tray to make sure there was nothing embarrassing on it, like cooked carrots or a fruit cup. It looked okay.

And right there in front of Charles W. Lister's smiling portrait, I was invited to sit at the vending machine tables. I mean, it wasn't a formal invitation delivered on a silver platter or anything. Dave didn't say, *Come join the popular kids next to the Cheetos.* He just nodded in the direction of the vending machines and said, "Some of us sit over there if you're looking for a table." And then he headed that way.

It took me a few minutes to decide whether or not the invitation was good for that particular day—or some future date. Kind of like those coupons you get at amusement parks: *good on your next visit.* Would I look desperate if I raced over to the table right after being invited? Or if I waited a day or two, would the guy forget he had invited me?

Note to self: If you wait, there is also the possibility that your next game could be a complete disaster. You could trip over home plate or something.

I casually headed toward the tables, hoping somebody would spot me and wave me to an open seat. Nobody did. Dave was sitting in the middle of a table directly in front of the soda machine. The words ICE-COLD PEPSI were right above his head. Six or seven other guys sat around him.

"Can I sit here?" I asked a guy on the end who was chugging a carton of chocolate milk and had four more lined up next to his tray.

"What?" The guy turned toward me with an annoyed expression. The kind of look you would give an irritating fly that had suddenly begun buzzing around your food. My hands began to sweat as they held tighter to my tray and I looked for a way out. Could I do a quick reverse and say, *uh, sorry, wrong table?*

But then Dave stood up and pointed in my direction. "It's Boston dude," he hollered. "Have a seat. Everybody move over so he can sit down." The chocolate milk guy used his arm to slide his milk cartons over and clear a space on the end. I squeezed in with my tray balanced precariously on the edge of the table, half on, half off. With my right arm clamped firmly down on the side of the tray to keep it anchored to the table, I had no idea how I was actually going to eat anything on it.

Dave Ernst (that was the last name printed on the back of his jersey) introduced me by saying I was the guy who had hit a baseball straight at Dog Face. Everybody at the table busted up laughing. "Really, you hit one at Dog Face?" The chocolate milk guy turned toward me, suddenly interested.

"Over his head," I answered. "Not really at him." I'm not sure why I thought this was an important point to make because nobody else really seemed to care. Just the fact that the dog-collar guy ended up on his butt in the grass and I scored a home run was all that mattered, it seemed. So, after a while, I just went along with Dave's version of what happened.

It felt strange to be the center of attention all of a sudden, though—to be asked about Boston and the teams I played on back there—but it was kind of reassuring, too. In Boston, I was used to sitting at a table of guys and talking about normal, everyday stuff. A few weeks of sitting by myself and having silent conversations with my lunch had been enough for me. Although I had to admit I was a little surprised by how *easy* it had been to get to the vending machine tables. Only one well-placed home run and I had somehow landed in the prime seats at Listerine.

It would have been a lot tougher at my Boston school. You had to be on the right teams and have the right friends. Just smacking a few hits in gym class wouldn't cut it.

Glancing around, I noticed how things looked different from the vending machine vantage point, too. For one, it seemed brighter and cleaner. This may have been due to the fact that there was a glass-enclosed courtyard close by.

The doors of the courtyard were propped open slightly, so breezy gusts of air and a few dry leaves swirled inside.

Being next to the machines also had other advantages. It seemed to be the custom for the guys at my table to buy a few snacks to share with the rest of the group. So a shiny brown bag of M&M's or a pack of mini Oreos could come shooting past you at any moment, scattering pieces as it traveled. If you sat at the end of the table, you were the one who had to be prepared to catch the item and keep it from plunging into oblivion. Then you sent the bag sliding back down the length of the table for everybody to take seconds.

I was so focused on not messing up my snack-catching job that when the bell rang at the end of lunch I realized I hadn't eaten any food on my tray except for a handful of potato chips and part of a chocolate chip cookie. Still, I felt as if things had gone almost perfectly. Let's just say Ivory's horoscope book probably couldn't have predicted a better day for Josh Greenwood. First, a home run. Then an invitation to become the newest member of the vending machine tables. The planets and stars were definitely on my side.

Until I got home. Then I got a third unexpected surprise. Which may have been the one the zodiac book was warning me about after all.

20. Watch Out for an Unexpected Surprise

My dad was mowing the lawn when I got home from school. This, by itself, was not unusual. September in Chicago had been pretty warm, so the grass was still growing fast. As I walked down the street, I could hear the uneven roaring of Dad's old mower going back and forth. Every time the ancient mower seemed on the verge of conking out, Dad had to speed up to keep the motor going.

He was finishing a row and getting ready to continue down the next patch of grass when he must have spotted me out of the corner of his eye. As I came walking up the driveway, he stopped and turned off the motor—which was something he almost never did, if he could help it. The sudden silence made my stomach lurch a little toward my throat, and the first thought that popped into my head was that my dad had some bad news about my grandma to share. Had she gotten worse? Had something else happened to her? But as my dad came closer, I was relieved to see his expression didn't look like anything serious had happened.

"How was school?" he asked, mopping his face with the bottom half of his shirt.

"Okay, fine," I said with a shrug, although I felt like shouting that it had been A GREAT DAY. That I wasn't a loser. That I had hit a ball out of the park. (Okay, into the weed-infested outfield at Charles Lister.) That I was now sitting at the vending machine tables. That Dog Face had fallen on his butt. However, none of these details—well, except for the home run—were the kinds of things a parent would understand and bringing them up would probably lead to more questions than I wanted to answer. That's why I kept my mouth shut.

"Guess what?" My dad rubbed his hands together. "I've got good news."

I eyed my dad cautiously, knowing it had to be something about Elvis: a new gig or a special event because that was the only good news he cared about.

"The music director called me today about something at your school—"

And this was the moment when things began to get hazy, literally. The sun suddenly felt blazing hot on my face and I could feel a trickle of sweat start creeping down my back. "What about school?" I said, dropping my backpack beside my feet.

"They want me to perform there."

A boulder of dread slammed into my stomach. "What?"

"They're going to be doing some kind of fifties concert at your school in November, and Viv told the music director about me, so he called this afternoon to ask if Elvis would be part of the show." Dad crossed his arms and grinned. "I said to him, 'Son, the King of Rock and Roll would be real proud to come and sing a few numbers for your program. Just gimme the word and I'll be there.' "

I wanted to die. Really, if a bolt of lightning would have come out of the clear blue sky right then, I wouldn't have gotten out of the way. I would have stood there with a big metal pole in my hand and said, *just hit me.*

Signs of the zodiac, signs of the zodiac
The future is in those little
signs of the zodiac . . .
—"Signs of the Zodiac," 1969

21. Words

Who was to blame? Lying flat on my bed staring up at my bumpy white bedroom ceiling, I decided the concert had to be Ivory's idea. Or partly her idea. Her mom had made the phone call to the music director, right? And Ivory was the one who had told me to watch out for an "unexpected surprise." She and her mom had probably planned the whole thing.

Well, it wasn't going to work. I swung my legs off the bed and headed into the kitchen to get the Viv's Vintage number from the scrap of cardboard that served as my dad's "important phone numbers" list. After a few rings, Ivory answered the phone. She sounded busy, as if there was a mad rush on disco pants or tie-dyed shirts. "Viv's Vintage, where you never go out of style. . . ."

I didn't even bother to say who it was. Let her figure it out. "You knew about my dad being invited to be Elvis at school, didn't you?" If a voice could be cold, mine would have been like those mammoths they find frozen in the ice in Siberia. A frozen mammoth voice.

Ivory pretended to be clueless and said she had no idea what I was talking about.

"Well, thanks, I appreciate it," I continued. "I spend a whole Saturday helping in your mom's store. For *free*, by the way. And then you go and tell everybody at school about my dad, so now the whole entire place will know about him being Elvis. I mean, why not?" My voice was getting louder and I had the feeling that maybe I wasn't making as much sense as I wanted to, but I kept going. "Just go ahead and make me look like a complete freak, just like you and all your dog-collar friends—"

Ivory interrupted again to say she had no idea what I meant.

"Ask your mom," I said, and slammed the phone down.

This was the first time I had ever hung up on somebody because I was mad. My mom would say it was totally out of character for me. Maybe it was. I mean, my friends and I goof around on the phone all the time and cut each other off in the middle of our conversations. Brian is especially famous for doing that—you'll be telling him a story and he'll say, "Another call, gotta go," and *click*, he's gone. Half the time he doesn't bother to call back, either. But I had never hung up on somebody on purpose. Until now.

The phone rang again about five minutes later.

"Did we get cut off?" Ivory asked sharply.

"Sure," I answered.

"Okay, well then," she continued, "I'm calling back because if you were referring to your dad and the school concert, I didn't have anything to do with it. My mom was the one who suggested it to the music director a while ago—not me, so don't blame me." She hurried on without even taking a breath. "And I don't appreciate you talking about my friends that way. Digger said you were a real jerk to him today in gym class. I don't know what's up with you, but I'm just calling to tell you that I don't care if your dad is dating my mom. I don't deserve to be treated like this and my friends don't, either, so just"—the voice paused as if searching for the right words—"get a life."

Then I think Ivory hung up on me, because there was a click and a dial tone. I tossed the phone onto the pillow and flopped back down on my bed to stare at the ceiling again. It hadn't changed much. Same ceiling fan. Same bumpy white plaster that looked like a really bad rash.

What were my options now? Clearly, calling Ivory had solved absolutely nothing. If she was telling the truth that the whole thing was Viv's idea, what could I do? Call Viv and ask her to uninvite my dad? They were "dating," so there was no way Viv would tell him he couldn't be part of the event.

What if I told him instead?

I tried to picture myself jogging out to the yard and telling my dad that I had given it a little thought and, hey, I didn't think it was a smart idea for him to perform at my school—that it would be best if he backed out of doing the show for his own good, for my own good, and just for the general good of society.

God. I rubbed my eyes in frustration. I didn't want to hurt my dad's feelings, I just wanted him to get a clue. I mean, why couldn't he see how this would humiliate both of us? Didn't he remember what middle school was like?

I could just imagine the entire Charles W. Lister auditorium full of kids staring at my forty-year-old dad as he came strutting onstage with his black leather outfit and gold chains and chest hair and orange makeup and sunglasses. He would start twisting his hips and singing "Hound Dog" or something like that, and the kids would collapse into hysterics. Or worse yet, what if they started booing and yelling things at him like, *Get off the stage, loser*? Think about how it sounds when an entire gymnasium is booing the ref during a basketball game. Now imagine it isn't a basketball game but your dad.

And once word got out that Elvis was my dad— because Ivory would probably blab to somebody who would blab to somebody else and soon the news would spread through the entire school—can you guess what it would be like to go to the cafeteria for lunch? Forget the vending machine tables, I wouldn't even be able to sit at the garbage can tables.

I clenched my hands over my eyes and tried to force myself to think more calmly. There had to be a way out. A way to keep my dad from performing that wouldn't hurt anybody's feelings. A way to keep myself from being humiliated. . . .

Looking back, I believe this was the point where I went wrong. It was impossible not to hurt somebody. There's a line in an Elvis song about being caught in a trap with no way out. Just like in the song, I was caught. And there was no good way out. Somebody was going to get hurt by whatever I did. It was just a matter of who would be hurt the most.

22. Sweepstakes

As it turned out, the idea for how to keep my dad from performing came from an unusual place: Gladys. A few days after I'd found out about my dad's Elvis gig, I was walking home from school when Gladys flagged me down outside her house. She said she had a letter she wanted me to read.

"I've got something I need you to look at, dear," Gladys called out from her porch, where she was standing in a rose-flowered housecoat and pink slippers. Once I got to her door, she held an envelope toward me. "This letter came in the mail today," she whispered in an excited voice. "It says I've won a million dollars. A million dollars—my stars, can you believe that?"

Of course, once I looked at the letter I knew exactly what it was. The metallic gold print at the top actually said GLADYS BEDFORD, YOU MAY BE OUR NEXT MILLION-DOLLAR SWEEPSTAKES WINNER. However, you had to send in your name and address in order to be entered in a drawing for the prize. Most of the important information about your chances of winning or not winning was in microscopic blocks of print at the bottom of the page.

Standing uncomfortably on Gladys's porch, I tried to figure out the nicest way to explain to her that she hadn't won any money. "I know the letter says you're a million-dollar winner, but that's not really what the letter means," I began. "It's a contest, see, where you send in an entry and you get entered into a drawing with millions of other people and somebody in the drawing wins a million dollars."

"So I didn't win all that money?"

I shook my head. "I mean, you have a chance—"

"Well, shoot," Gladys interrupted. "And there I was thinking I was gonna die a rich old lady. That's the way life goes, though. Easy come, easy go." She waved her hand in the air. "How about coming in for a drink of something before you leave?"

I didn't really want to stay, but I felt like Gladys had been disappointed enough for one day, so I told her a glass of water would be fine but I couldn't stay very long. While I was sitting at her kitchen table, my eyes glanced over the sweepstakes letter again.

GLADYS BEDFORD, YOU MAY BE OUR NEXT . . .

And I started thinking about what would happen if my dad got the same kind of letter. What if he actually won a

150

million dollars, for instance? Would he give up being Elvis? Would it stop him from performing at my school?

That's when the idea hit me. Well, no, it wasn't like *bam, here's an idea*—it was more like in the game of Solitaire when you turn a card over and you don't see where it fits at first and then all of a sudden you do. And once that card is moved into the right spot, a lot of other cards fall into place.

What if my dad received his own sweepstakes letter? Not a letter offering him a million dollars, but one that invited him to enter a special Elvis competition in Chicago? And what if the contest was on the same day as the school show?

JERRY DENNY, YOU HAVE THE CHANCE TO BE OUR NEXT CHICAGO ELVIS. . . .

It was exactly the kind of opportunity that would appeal to my dad. He was always looking for bigger and better places to perform. And if it was on the same day as the school event, he'd definitely go ahead and cancel the school gig. Maybe the contest could even offer the winner the chance to compete in Las Vegas at a national—no, *international*—Elvis competition with the best Elvises from all over the world.

The only drawback I could see was the fact that there wasn't going to be a real competition. But I thought I could solve that problem by sending another letter later on—maybe a week or so before the competition date—saying the show had been canceled but would be rescheduled at a later time.

The beauty of my plan was that it didn't really hurt anybody. The school wouldn't be hurt—they would have plenty of time to find another Elvis to perform. My dad's feelings wouldn't be hurt by standing in front of a crowd of howling, jeering middle school kids. And I wouldn't be hurt by people finding out who he was.

Sure, it required being a little dishonest. But *in theory* (my Listerine science teacher's favorite phrase) my idea was no different than a sweepstakes letter telling people "you may be a winner." My dad *might* be the winner of a Chicago Elvis contest, if it actually happened. Only it wouldn't. And even if he was a little disappointed when the contest was canceled, it still wasn't as bad as being publicly humiliated. Being disappointed was like going to the store and discovering they were sold out of your favorite ice cream flavor. No big deal. You got over it.

However, being publicly humiliated was way worse. Especially if you were my dad and you hadn't been to middle school in, oh, about twenty-seven years and you had no idea what you were getting into when you agreed to perform in front of hundreds of sixth, seventh, and eighth graders. So by writing the letter, I swear I believed I was saving him from being hurt.

What I didn't consider at the time was the effect the letter would have on somebody like my dad—somebody who thinks he always has a chance in life, no matter what the odds are. My dad is the kind of person who would actually believe he could be a MILLION-DOLLAR WINNER, while my mom and I would just laugh and toss the letter in the trash. Since I didn't think about how seriously my dad might take the whole idea, I didn't realize what was totally wrong with my plan.

The other mistake I made was taking the idea too far. Once I started putting my ideas down on paper, I couldn't stop. I'm kind of ashamed to admit it now, but I had a lot of fun creating the Elvis letter on my computer. It took me about three days to pull together the whole page. I found a great black-and-white clip art picture of Elvis in his younger years, and I put that in the upper left corner of the invitation. Across the top, I typed: CALLING ALL CHICAGO ELVISES! A ONCE-IN-A-LIFETIME OPPORTUNITY! YOU MAY BE THE NEXT LAS VEGAS ELVIS!

Note: If some of the words have a familiar ring, it's because I borrowed a few of them from Gladys's sweepstakes letter.

Searching through the Chicago Yellow Pages, I found a fancy downtown hotel to use as the site for the contest: the InterContinental Hotel with the Grand Ballroom. That sounded convincing enough to me. Who wouldn't give up a crummy middle school program at Charles W. Lister for the opportunity to perform at the Grand Ballroom? And just to be sure the whole plan would work, I listed five thousand dollars as the first prize—with the chance to be part of a special Las Vegas Elvis concert.

I had to admit, it looked completely professional when I was finished. I even added a few lines of microscopic type at the bottom: THE INTERCONTINENTAL HOTEL AND ITS EMPLOYEES ARE NOT LIABLE FOR THE JUDGING OR OUTCOME OF THE ELVIS CONTEST. ALL DECISIONS BY THE ELVIS JUDGES ARE FINAL. NO REFUNDS OR EXCHANGES.

Note: I was very proud of the word "liable."

I mailed the letter in the blue post office mailbox across from Charles Lister. As I pulled back the handle of the mailbox and watched the envelope slide down the metal chute, I felt like a big weight had been lifted off my shoulders. Three days of work with fonts and mailing labels and spell-checking everything about a hundred times—and now the letter was done and out of my hands. Calling all Chicago Elvises. . . .

I gave a letter to the postman

He put it in his sack . . .

—"Return to Sender," 1962

23. Return to Sender

A few days later, the letter arrived at my dad's house—or *returned* to it (depending on your perspective). But I have to say I was a little shocked when I got home from school and found my dad sitting in the living room, wearing a suit and tie. "Put on something nice," he announced excitedly, jumping up from the sofa as I came through the door. "I'm taking us downtown for dinner tonight."

"Us?"

"You and me." My dad patted my back. "I'm in the mood for a celebration."

I could feel a small prickling start in my scalp and make its way down the back of my neck. You know the feeling you get when you are caught in the middle of telling a big fat juicy lie to your parents? When you can't decide whether to stop or keep going with your story?

"What are we celebrating?" I said, trying to appear clueless, even though I had already guessed.

"Just something good that happened to me today. You'll see . . . ," my dad said with a secretive smile. "I don't want to give it away just yet."

As I stood in my bedroom pulling on a new pair of khakis that my mom had sent the week before with an update about my grandma, I had to admit that my dad's reaction wasn't exactly what I'd been expecting. I tried to decide how to act when my dad told me about the letter.

Surprised? Of course surprised. But since the contest wasn't going to happen, I didn't want to encourage him too much—especially since I hadn't shown much interest in his Elvis gigs before. Maybe I needed to play it cool. Say something like, *that's great—but the competition will probably be pretty tough, won't it?* Mostly I just hoped the whole conversation would end quickly, because I wasn't very good at any of this deep psychological stuff.

It took about forty minutes to get downtown from my dad's neighborhood. We drove past the InterContinental Hotel with the Grand Ballroom on our way to the restaurant. Dad leaned toward my window and pointed out the white-gloved guy standing by the hotel's gold-and-glass front doors. "Look, they even have somebody to open the doors for you at that place. Fancy-schmancy, huh?"

"Yeah, pretty nice," I said, pretending to seem more interested in cracking my knuckles than in what was going on outside.

My dad had made reservations at a Chinese restaurant near the hotel, although, by the empty look of the place, he didn't need to bother. It was kind of embarrassing to watch him march right up to the front desk with his slicked-back hair and his suit and announce, "Reservation for Denny—two people" when most of the tables didn't have a soul sitting at them. The Chinese lady at the front pretended to take him seriously by spending a few minutes paging through a black book on the desk before saying, "Ah yes, Mr. Denny, we have a table for you. Right this way."

We were taken to a white-cloth-covered table by a window facing a brick wall. It was a nicely made brick wall but not exactly what you would call a view. I don't think my dad noticed the window or the lack of a view, though. After we sat down, Dad reached into his pocket and set an envelope on the table in front of me. "Guess what came in the mail today?" he said excitedly. "Open it up and look."

I could feel the prickly needles creeping up the back of my neck as I slid the letter I had written out of the envelope. I could practically recite what it said, word for word, from memory: Calling All Chicago Elvises! A Once-in-a-Lifetime Opportunity! You May Be the Next . . .

As I pretended to be slowly reading the letter, I wondered how I could possibly look up again without appearing guilty. This was the part of the plan that I hadn't considered. I hadn't expected my dad to be sitting two feet away, studying my face while I read my own words.

"This sounds pretty good," I said, folding up the letter and avoiding his eyes.

"It's the same day as the concert at your school, though."

I shrugged, trying to play it cool. "So cancel the school thing. The contest is more of a big deal than coming to a school concert, right?" I was amazed at how smoothly these words came out of my mouth.

Note to self: Maybe you should consider a career in Hollywood.

A grin spread across my dad's face and he leaned forward, jostling the table with his elbows. The lighted candle on the table flickered. "You and I must be on the same page. That's exactly what I thought, too." His voice dropped to a whisper, as if someone in the empty restaurant might overhear us talking. "This could be my big break, you know. If I win this competition and get to go to Vegas—man, that would be it!" His voice rose excitedly. "If people know you're good, you can make big money traveling around the country being Elvis."

My throat began to feel like I had swallowed a mouthful

of sand. I reached for one of the water glasses on the table and took a long drink. The glass wobbled in my hand as I set it back down and little splashes seeped into the table-cloth.

The Chinese lady came back with two menus. "Any questions—be back in few minutes," she said, handing them to us with a polite smile.

"Get whatever you want," my dad said, passing one to me. "I'm feeling lucky tonight."

It got worse. All through dinner, he talked about how he was going to prepare for the competition. "My costume needs work, that's the first thing," he said, shoveling big spoonfuls of rice into his mouth. "My shoes aren't the right color. Elvis wore white, so I've gotta find some white boots somewhere, and I need something flashier than the black leather costume I've been wearing. Something from Elvis's later years. Gotta do a lot more practicing on the moves, too. I just can't get the leg shake exactly the way he did it, no matter how much I keep working on it."

And right there in the middle of Ho Wah's nice, quiet (and fortunately empty) restaurant, my dad had to show me the secret of how Elvis jiggled his leg. "I'll show you what I mean—"

"Dad, jeez, come on—"

"No, I'm serious. It's a really simple move. Look how

he did it." My dad stood up. "It's a heel tap, not a toe tap, see—" His heel began bouncing up and down on the red carpet as if he had suddenly stepped on a poisonous snake. Or a nest of ground wasps. "But whenever I'm performing, I always start tapping my toes instead, which looks completely wrong, doesn't it? It doesn't have the same leg jiggle, does it?"

I could not believe we were actually having a demonstration of "leg jiggles" in the middle of a Chinese restaurant.

As my dad's shoe tapped one way and then the other on the thick red carpet, I could see the Chinese lady hurrying across the room toward us. Dad, who was totally oblivious to everything, slid back into his seat and picked up his white napkin, which had fallen on the floor. "So I've gotta get that move right before the competition," he said, dumping another huge pile of rice onto his plate. "And I keep messing up the timing on the song 'Teddy Bear.' 'Just wanna be' "—he tapped two fingers on the table and hummed in a low voice—" 'your Teddy Bear.' See, that pause is tough."

The Chinese lady came over, looking worried. "Everything okay?"

My dad nodded and answered through a mouthful of food that the meal was great. I could see the Chinese lady's eyes glance toward my plate, where I had only made a few dents in my chicken fried rice mountain. A sharp throbbing pain had started right below my ribs.

Driving back in the car with my dad, I had a lot of time to think. Or at least the guilty side of my brain had a lot of time to think. As the lights of the city flashed past the car windows, I noticed how everything had a hazy, starburst kind of look—the streetlights, the neon signs, the crosswalk signals—as if I was seeing Chicago underwater.

Note: I knew this was an observation that shouldn't be shared with any adult in my life because it might mean I would eventually need glasses.

Next to me, my dad hummed songs to himself and drummed his fingers on the steering wheel, as if he was rehearsing his entire Elvis show in his head from start to finish. I could tell he was in a really good mood. This made the guilty voices in my brain even louder. And the stomach pain sharper.

Even then, I sensed that something about my plan wasn't working. Like the city skimming by the car windows, something, somewhere, seemed to have gone hazily wrong. I just didn't know what it was.

24. Blue Hawaii

The wrongness seemed to get worse as the weeks passed. My dad spent hours in his bedroom watching old tapes of Elvis concerts to practice the "moves," as he called them: the body shake, the arm pump, the pinwheel, the karate chop. He would dance in front of a tall mirror that leaned against one of his bedroom walls. Lying in my bed at night, I could hear his feet moving on the floor right above my head, jiggling back and forth to *Elvis: The Great Performances* boxed set or who knows what else.

At the same time all of this was happening, I had plenty of things in my own life to be worrying about—namely the fact that my grandma wasn't getting better as fast as my mom had hoped and my friends from Boston appeared to have completely forgotten about me. Well, that's not quite true. Brian was still forwarding his usual stuff: pictures of goats born with two heads, or people who had gotten their arms stuck in public toilets. But nobody else from Boston had answered my e-mail messages in about a month. As the end of October arrived, it looked as if I'd be lucky if I ever got to go home.

When my mom phoned one Saturday afternoon, I tried asking her how much longer she thought it would be. It was her usual "check up on Josh" call. Every Saturday, and two or three times during the week, she'd call to see how everything was going in Chicago.

"How much longer will *what* be?" she replied in a harried-sounding voice. In the background, you could hear the whine of power tools as workers installed special railings and ramps in my grandma's trailer, for whenever she was finally able to come back to Shadyside Villas. I had to repeat my question three times before my mom got it.

"You need to understand that somebody her age takes a long time to recover," my mom said with a tired sigh. "I know it's hard, Josh, but she's making more progress every day, and we just have to be patient and wait. Okay? Everything will be back to normal soon, I promise." And then I could hear the sound of a doorbell ringing and she had to hang up.

After my mom's phone call, I decided to take a walk. Just to be somewhere other than my dad's house in Chicago, even if being outside wasn't much farther away than being inside. It was a start at least. My dad was in the kitchen working on one of his speakers that had started to buzz. He'd been focused on the speaker for two days. It was all he'd been talking about—was it a serious buzz, was it a minor buzz, was it a noticeable buzz, was it an expensive-to-fix buzz—and I was really sick of hearing about the buzzing speaker, so I didn't bother to tell him I was leaving.

Outside, the sky was a gloomy gray color and the air was cold. It was the end of October, but it felt like January. Stuffing my hands deep into the front pockets of my jeans and holding my arms against my sides for warmth, I probably looked like some kind of frozen robot person as I walked stiffly up one side of the deserted street, past Gladys's house and the other aluminum-awning houses. Then back down the opposite side.

A brown UPS truck drove past me, kicking up piles of leaves as it went by. I was surprised to see it turn and pull into my dad's driveway. What was the truck delivering to us? When I got back about fifteen minutes later, I found out. As I closed the front door, my dad called out from the living room, "Hey, Josh, come in here. I've got something to show you."

That was the moment when the wrongness got worse. Much worse.

Imagine walking into the living room to find your dad (who you had last seen crouched over a dismantled speaker

165

in torn jeans and an old '80s concert T-shirt) now dressed in a blinding white jumpsuit and cape, which are completely covered with gold stars and colored glass rhinestones.

"What the heck—" I said, totally shocked.

Note: It may not have been "heck" that I said. I'm not exaggerating, my dad looked like he had just flown in from the planet Krypton.

"Man, isn't this something?" Dad held his arms out and turned around slowly so I could get the full rhinestone effect. The costume's tall white collar came up to his chin. Blue and red glass rhinestones, hundreds of them, formed the outstretched wings of a large eagle on the front of the jumpsuit. Two rows of gold stars trailed down the white arms of the costume, and there was a line of smaller rhinestone eagles along each of the flared polyester pant legs, which ended kind of abruptly at my dad's bare feet. "Have you ever seen an outfit like this one before?"

I couldn't even get an answer out.

"It's called the Aloha Eagle," my dad continued proudly. "All the best impersonators have one. Elvis wore it for his 1973 television special from Hawaii. Get it? Aloha and"—he pointed to the large rhinestone bird stretched across his chest—"Eagle."

The entire time my dad was talking, I could feel a sickening storm beginning to brew in my stomach. You know

166

the feeling you get after you guzzle a 42-ounce soda and then get into a car and ride down a bumpy road in the backseat? That was the feeling I had as I looked at the costume. Because I knew exactly what he had gotten it for. And I had a pretty good guess it wasn't free. But the feeling in my stomach forced me to ask, just to find out for sure.

"One thousand five hundred bucks," Dad said, leaning on one knee and demonstrating an Elvis arm thrust. "How's that for a deal? The way I figured it, I had to take a chance in this business if I wanted to get ahead. And if this jumpsuit doesn't put Jerry Denny in the running for a trip to Vegas, I mean, what else will?" He stood up and stretched out his arms. "Look at me, Josh, don't I look like the King?"

A huge smile spread across my dad's face as he stood there, absolutely convinced he was the perfect Elvis and he was going to win the trip to Las Vegas—and if there had been music playing, this would have been the point with the big, happy crescendo. But instead, there was just the silent sound of my brain screaming that all of this was my fault.

"It looks great," I managed to say, and then I took off, because if I stayed one minute longer looking at my dad's clueless smile and the fifteen-hundred-dollar rhinestone eagle glinting in the living room light, the storm in my stomach was going to come lurching out of me.

In my bedroom, I closed the door and flopped down in the middle of the old blue shag carpet. Pressing my arms across my face, I tried to decide whether it would be better to pack up my stuff and leave now or later. Should I call my mom and beg her for a plane ticket to Florida? No questions asked? Could I tell her it was an emergency? Could I leave Chicago that night?

Then I began to get angry at my dad, because, looking at it another way, the whole situation was his fault. Why did I have to feel guilty? Was it really *my* fault he'd decided to buy some Aloha costume? Or that he had believed every word of my letter? It hadn't said to go out and blow a fortune on a new jumpsuit, had it? That was completely my dad's own choice, wasn't it?

The tug-of-war over who was more wrong—me for coming up with the whole idea or my dad for believing it—jerked back and forth in my head. *Dad. Me. Dad. Me.* Mostly, I think I kept focusing on who deserved the most blame because it was a good way to avoid worrying about the problem of what I was going to do next.

I ended up wimping out and calling Ivory. After spending
an hour trying to come up with the name of somebody to
call—like those phone-a-friends you can use if you're on a
game show and stuck on the million-dollar question—I
couldn't think of anybody else to ask for advice. How sad
is that? Nobody back in Boston knew about my dad being
Elvis, and the guys at Listerine thought I was Josh
Greenwood, completely normal person. I even considered
going down the street to talk to Gladys. But she had been
acting kind of mixed-up lately, and I didn't want to make
her more confused.

So I dialed Viv's Vintage with no idea of what to say to
Ivory. Or how to keep her from hanging up. Ever since I'd
blamed her for my dad being invited to the school concert,
she'd been avoiding me. Going out of her way to avoid
me, actually. For instance, if we happened to be passing

169

through the hallway at the same time, she would cut across to the other side. It reminded me of that experiment where you put pepper flakes in a dish with some water and then stick a bar of soap in the dish and the pepper flakes zoom to the other side.

Ivory answered the phone with the usual overly cheerful, overly hopeful Viv's Vintage greeting. Since it was Saturday afternoon, I figured the store was probably empty.

"How's it going?" I said in a voice that was meant to sound friendly.

"Who is this?"

"Josh Greenwood."

There was a long, uncomfortable pause. "Do you want something?" Ivory's sharp voice finally interrupted the silence. "Because I'm busy, even if you're not."

Right at that point, I had this insane desire to start laughing. Have you ever been in a situation where everything is tense and sad, like at a funeral, and suddenly you feel like this horrible laugh wants to come exploding out of you? Not a happy laugh, but a desperate, possessed kind of laugh you can't stop? That's the way I felt right at that moment, as if I was going to start insanely laughing, even though that was the exact opposite of how I felt.

"I need to talk to you about something with my dad." I managed to get these words out of my mouth in one fast, mumbled sentence, without any hysterical laughter breaking out.

"About what?"

"He's here right now. I can't really talk," I lied.

I think Ivory only agreed to meet with me because she thought it had something to do with our parents' relationship. "I'll meet you in an hour at the little park near the shoe store where your dad worked," she said impatiently.

"The park?" I couldn't recall any parks.

"It's small. Look for the iron gate. And the bus shelter out front. If you can't find it, ask somebody." And that's all the information I could get out of Ivory.

So for the second time that day, I headed down Oakmont—although this time I was smart enough to bring along a jacket. It took me about forty-five minutes to walk all the way to the park with Chicago's arctic wind whipping my face.

Note to self: Learn how to ride the city bus.

The park turned out to be pretty close to Murphy's Shoes. Squeezed along the busy street and surrounded by a spiked fence, it didn't exactly cry out "environmental paradise," however. Two rusted swing sets sat in the middle of a dusty bowl of dirt. There were a few of those riding animals for little kids—the ones on those big metal springs that sway back and forth. One of the springs was missing

171

an animal, as if it had decided *the heck with this* and taken off.

Ivory was nowhere in sight. I began to wonder if sending me to sit in a deserted park was her idea of a cruel joke. But then I spotted somebody pedaling quickly down the street on a bicycle. From a distance, she looked like she had a white squirrel draped across her shoulders, but as Ivory got closer, I could see the squirrel was actually a fur-type collar attached to an old leather coat. Close up, her jacket reminded me of something Amelia Earhart would wear to fly across the Atlantic. All she needed was a pair of goggles.

"Hey," Ivory said, bumping her bike across the uneven ground and stopping in front of me. "You found it."

"Yeah." I stuffed my cold hands in my pockets, feeling uncomfortable.

"Where do you want to talk?"

I shrugged. "Wherever. Your choice."

Looking around at the choices—(a) swing set, (b) giant metal spring animals, or (c) benches in need of a good paint job—Ivory picked the benches. She perched on the end of one and I sat on the end of another. There was a small canyon of dirt and leaves and people's discarded cigarette butts between us.

"So," Ivory said, crossing her legs and giving me a frown. "What's up?"

Honestly, I still hadn't figured out how much I was

going to tell her. I started by explaining how I was having some problems with my dad (without going into any specifics)—how I'd written a letter that had made things a lot worse. "Now I'm kinda stuck about what to do next," I finished.

Ivory squinted at me. "I have absolutely no idea what you're talking about."

Glancing at the old tree above us (which might have been prettier earlier in the fall, but now its leaves were a sad yellow-brown color), I decided I really couldn't stand keeping the whole story to myself one minute longer. Even if the person who heard it turned around and told a hundred other people. Even if the person was Ivory.

So I just spilled my guts right there in the middle of that empty, freezing cold park. I told Ivory everything: about the letter, the Grand Ballroom, the five-thousand-dollar prize, even the Aloha Eagle. After I was done, she didn't say a word at first. Shaking her head, she finally said, "Wow, that is really twisted."

"Thanks." I looked up and glared at her. "That helps."

Ivory picked up a leaf from the bench and twirled the stem in her hand. "I just can't believe you would do some-thing like that. I mean"—she paused and shrugged—"your dad seems like such a cool person to have for a father. I wouldn't even think of doing something like that to my mom . . . ," her voice trailed off.

"Thanks. That helps more."

After that, it was quiet for about five minutes. You could hear the cars zipping by the front of the park and a jet going overhead. "So do you have any ideas," I mumbled finally, "about how to get out of this?" Trying to ignore the stinging sensation starting in the corners of my eyes, I pretended to be interested in watching the cars passing by on the street.

"Other than telling your dad what you did?"

"Yeah."

"Not that I can think of, no."

"So what do I say? 'Sorry you blew fifteen hundred bucks on a costume, Dad'? He's been practicing for weeks. He really believes he's going to Las Vegas." My voice rose and fell in odd, uncontrollable ways like a squeaky instrument. "He's gonna hate me for the rest of his life when he finds out what I did. *God*"—I kicked at the patch of dirt and stones under my feet—"everything in my life is such a total freaking mess right now."

Ivory stood up suddenly and brushed the scraps of torn leaves off her jeans. "I can't stay and talk any longer. I've gotta get back to the store and help out my mom."

I looked up, kind of surprised by her sharp tone. "What?"

"No matter what you talk about, it's always about you, isn't it?" Ivory glared at me. Her voice grew louder and more impatient. "What if your dad hates you, what if you

174

have to pay him back for his costume, what if he embarrasses you, what if people find out he's Elvis, what if your popular jock friends at Listerine don't let you hang out with them anymore—everything is always about you, isn't it?"

Ivory yanked her bike up from where it lay on its side. "Maybe you should spend some time walking around in other people's feet for a while," she snapped over her shoulder, and then she abruptly headed out, with her wheels wobbling across the sparse grass and through the iron gate.

Note to Ivory: The saying is "walk around in somebody else's *shoes*"—not feet.

Although the idea of walking around in somebody else's feet kind of cracked me up the more I thought about it. A fat gray pigeon was pecking for food around the park benches, which made me wonder how it might feel to walk around on a pigeon's skinny red feet. Or metal park animal springs: *bo-ing, bo-ing.* Or even—as a dog trotted past the park gate with its owner—fuzzy brown dog feet.

Of course, deep down, I knew what Ivory was trying to say. I just wasn't ready to admit to myself that maybe she had a point about seeing things from somebody else's eyes—or feet—sometimes.

But I figured she was right that it was time to tell my dad the truth about the letter. Before he bought another

Aloha costume or blew his *entire* life savings because of me. . . .

Still, it took me another day just to get up the nerve to talk to him. Even then, I probably should have waited a little longer and not rushed in, because nothing came out the way I had planned.

Wise men say

Only fools rush in . . .

—"Can't Help Falling in Love," 1961

26. Elvis Has Left the Building

It was about five o'clock on Sunday when I knocked on my dad's bedroom door. He'd been rehearsing all afternoon.

"Come on in," his voice called out.

Walking into his room was like entering an Elvis museum. You had to step over boxes of JERRY DENNY AS THE KING flyers and stacks of Elvis CDs and videos and piles of rainbow scarves. But the thing that got me every time was the life-size cutout of Elvis standing near my dad's closet door. Cardboard Elvis had been a gift to my dad from one of his friends, but it was so realistic-looking it made me jump every time I saw it. Like the King had suddenly materialized out of thin air to strum his guitar in my dad's bedroom.

"What's up?" My dad leaned over and switched off the music coming from the stack of stereo equipment next to one wall.

"It's something about school," I said. Stretching out across my dad's bed, I pretended to be interested in studying the ceiling. Better if I didn't look at my dad or Cardboard Elvis while I was talking.

Dad cleared aside some plastic CD cases and sat down on the edge of the bed. "What about school?" His fingers drummed against his legs as if he wasn't really paying attention but was still thinking about the song he'd been listening to when I walked in.

I tried to remember what I had planned to say, but once I started talking, none of the words came out the way I had practiced them. "Everybody thought I'd be okay with coming to Chicago and going to a new school, right?" I began in a fairly normal voice.

"I guess, sure," my dad said, giving me a puzzled look. "Why?"

"I was fine with coming here to your house for three or four months or whatever, until Grandma got better, right?"

My dad nodded slowly. "Sure, yes. . . ."

After that, my voice began to grow less sorry and more angry. It was like another thirteen-year-old suddenly took over my body: *Josh Greenwood, Now Being Played by His Evil Twin.* "Everybody thinks I can handle anything. No problem—send Josh to a new city or a new school or whatever, he'll be fine, right?"

My voice rushed on, gathering steam. "Then, just when he's starting to fit in with people and he's made, like, two or three friends . . . why not have his dad go ahead and screw it all up? Because Josh can handle anything, right? Don't even bother asking Josh his opinion—"

"What?" my dad interrupted, sounding completely surprised and confused. "What have I messed up? Tell me."

This was the point when one of those possessed, forced laughs came out. "Jeez, Dad, how can you not see it?" My voice rose, sounding embarrassingly like a girl's at one point. "Walking around pretending you're Elvis and buying thousand-dollar costumes—that's normal? And then you go and sign up to be Elvis at my school? I mean, what do you think I'd be upset about?"

None of this conversation was going the way I had planned.

"You know the letter you got about the Chicago Elvis contest?" I said. There was no stopping now.

My dad nodded. "Sure, yes."

"Well, I was the one who made up that letter, because if I hadn't, you would've just gone ahead and shown up at my school, right?" My arms gestured angrily at the air. "Who cares about asking me what I think? Nobody ever worries about that. Not you. Not Mom. Just go and embarrass me in front of the whole entire place."

I could hear Ivory's accusing voice in my head repeating: *It's always about you.* I knew that's the way it sounded, but I couldn't help it.

"You made up the letter about the contest?" My dad's voice was full of disbelief and something else I couldn't name, something deeper and more painful. I felt a thick lump rising in my throat as I said yes.

"There's no contest, no Las Vegas? Nothing? It was all a joke?"

"Not a joke—I just—"

"Just what?" My dad stared at me. "Thought you'd see what you could do for fun? Man"—he ran his fingers through his hair—"I thought you and I were way past this, Josh. I thought we were getting along better these days. I thought things had been kind of okay lately." Leaning over, he picked up his coat from the floor. "But I guess I was wrong, wasn't I?" Shaking his head, he said in a hurt voice, "Guess I was totally wrong."

And then he stood up, walked out of the room, and pulled the door shut behind him. He didn't just walk out of the bedroom, either. He left the house. I heard the front door slam and the sound of the car pulling out of the garage. The garage door thudded closed and then it was silent. Sitting by myself in his Elvis room, I couldn't keep my mind from replaying the whole scene—what he had said, what I had said, over and over—as if there was something I could change about it now. Only there wasn't. I had completely and totally screwed up this time. A book of Elvis sheet music was lying on the floor near my feet. It was open to the song "Heartbreak Hotel." Which seemed to fit the moment perfectly.

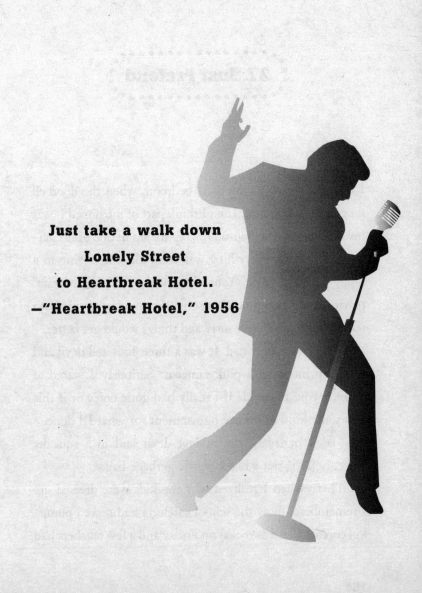

**Just take a walk down
Lonely Street
to Heartbreak Hotel.
—"Heartbreak Hotel," 1956**

27. Just Pretend

I was still sitting in my dad's bedroom when the doorbell rang about a half hour later. I think part of me hoped it was my dad and maybe he would wrap me up in one of his garlic hugs and say everything was okay, like the ending to a sappy Disney movie. You know, with "Hakuna Matata" playing in the background or something, and we would both tell each other we were sorry and things would get better.

But it wasn't my dad. It was a three-foot-tall devil and a fairy princess in a pink raincoat. Seriously. I stared at them, trying to decide if I really had gone crazy or if this was some kind of bizarre punishment for what I'd done.

"Trick or treat," the midget devil said in a squeaky voice, holding out a black plastic garbage bag.

That's when I realized why the kids were dressed up. I remembered how the school cafeteria had served pumpkin cookies (hard as rocks) on Friday and a few teachers had worn costumes. This weekend was Halloween. And there I was, standing in front of an open door with absolutely no candy to give out. What a complete moron I was.

I told the two kids to hang on.

"What?" The midget devil didn't seem to understand what I meant and glanced back at somebody who was standing in the darkness behind him, holding an umbrella.

"Hang on," I said louder. "I've gotta get some candy."

By some miracle, my dad had a bag of Snickers bars stashed in the back of his cereal cabinet. Who knows how long the candy bars had been there. Last Halloween? Christmas? I ripped open the bag and headed back to the front door. The devil and the fairy princess were in the middle of asking the adult behind them if they should go to the next house. "Maybe he's not coming back," the princess insisted.

Pulling out a handful of candy, I mumbled, "Happy Halloween."

As the Snickers bars landed softly on the heavy pile already inside their bags, the midget devil asked me where Elvis had gone.

"What?" I asked, not sure I'd heard him right.

The boy glanced back at the adult. "My dad says Elvis lives here."

I thought about answering that Elvis had left the building and probably wasn't ever coming back because

185

of me, but instead I told them he was at a gig. "He's got a show tonight, I think."

The adult in the darkness said, "Well, tell him the neighbors across the street—the ones that have the big cookout every year—said hello. Tell him we want tickets to see his act one of these days."

"Sure," I said. "I will."

After the devil and the princess disappeared into the rain, I closed the door and tried not to think about how my mom and I used to be just like those little kids and their parents. How we used to walk around on Halloween with our raincoats and our plastic garbage bags of candy.

I had been a baseball player for trick-or-treating in fourth grade. Which was the same year my mom had insisted that if I didn't feel comfortable wearing a "real" costume (she didn't consider my baseball uniform a real costume), I was getting too old for trick-or-treating. So fourth grade was the last year I went out for Halloween.

But honestly, I would have given anything to go trick-or-treating again. I could still remember how it felt to collect loads of candy and then spend hours sorting it into piles on the living room floor: the good candy, the okay candy, and the candy (black licorice) nobody would ever eat. I mean, those were the times when it was fun to be a kid. The older you got, the more the fun disappeared. Every year, something else was taken away.

Halloween had been one of the last things to go. What was left? Thanksgiving?

Even parents changed from nice, umbrella-toting people who held your hand and walked around with you in the dark (not that I wanted my hand held!) to complicated people who did things that didn't make sense anymore. They got divorced. They turned into Elvis. They went to Florida without you to take care of your grandma and her broken hip.

Standing there in the hallway with my bag of old and possibly expired Snickers, I just wanted to go back to the way things were. I was sick of being in Chicago. I was sick of being thirteen years old. I was sick of being Josh Greenwood.

My glance fell on my dad's new pair of Elvis boots sitting in the hallway. They were still in the same spot where he'd left them after coming back from a show the night before—one boot slightly ahead of the other, as if he had taken them off in midstep.

What was it Ivory had said? *You need to walk around in somebody else's feet for a while.* . . . And I thought—*what the heck.*

Call me completely insane, but even though I had nowhere to go, and nobody to go with, I decided to try being Elvis for Halloween. Just for fun. Just to pass out candy to the little kids. Why not? My dad already had the costume stuff, right? I would walk around in his shoes for a while. Literally.

Upstairs, I found a pair of my dad's gold Elvis sunglasses to wear. Using a brown eye pencil from his bathroom, I drew triangle sideburns on each side of my face and colored them in with little slashes to look like hair. Then I pulled on one of his black leather Elvis jackets. However, there was *no way* I was showing any part of my thirteen-year-old chest to the world, so the jacket went on over a dark blue T-shirt.

With the slightly large leather coat and the huge sunglasses, I thought I looked like a cross between Elvis and some bizarre insect. *Yes, Praying Mantis Elvis, that's me.* But the next little kid who came to my dad's door didn't seem to notice. When I opened the door, he cracked up and said, "Are you Elvis?"

Weirdly, I never had to explain who I was when people came to the door—everybody always knew. Even though I was a thirteen-year-old kid with gold sunglasses and fake sideburns drawn on my face with brown eye pencil, they thought it was a great costume. Some of the little kids even turned around and waved at me as they headed back into the darkness. "Bye, Elvis. . . ."

That's when I began to realize something about being Elvis: that who you are isn't as important as who you are trying to be.

28. Cheerleaders and Cowboys

When I was down to my last five Snickers bars, two people came walking up the rainy sidewalk to the house. Standing by the door, I didn't recognize them at first. I just thought they looked too tall and too old to be trick-or-treating. (My mom wouldn't have approved.) The guy was dressed like a cowboy, with a Western hat and a large red bandanna tied around his neck. The girl was wearing a cheerleader costume, complete with green-and-silver pom-poms. It took me a minute to realize that the two people coming up to my dad's porch were actually Digger and Ivory.

But I think Ivory was way more shocked than me.

"Josh?" She leaned forward to stare at me through the screen door and her voice fell to an incredulous whisper. "What are you doing?"

Until then, it hadn't occurred to me that anybody from

school might come by and see me handing out candy, dressed up as Elvis. I mean, who would expect a couple of Charles W. Lister seventh graders to be wandering around with the five-year-old fairy princesses and midget devils?

Feeling my face beginning to get warm, I tried to downplay the whole costume. "I'm just handing out candy to the little kids. For my dad," I added stupidly.

"Where is he?" Ivory asked, with a tone that suggested she hadn't forgotten our park conversation.

"He's got a gig."

Ivory gave me a closer look. "He didn't need his costume?"

Note to Ivory: What are you? The FBI cheerleader?

"It's an extra one," I said.

Slowly, Ivory's face broke into a smile. "Well, you look kind of deranged as Elvis. Deranged, but good. Right, Digger?"

Behind her, Cowboy Digger nodded. I shifted uncomfortably from one foot to the other, wondering how much longer they'd stick around on my dad's porch, talking to me through the screen door. "We aren't really trick-or-treating for candy this year," Ivory began explaining. "We're going around the neighborhood collecting money for Greenpeace. We stopped by because we thought maybe your dad might want to donate something."

"But hey, if you want to give us some candy bars instead, that's okay, too," Digger joked, gesturing at the almost empty Snickers bag I was still holding. "We're not that picky."

Somehow, I ended up sitting on my dad's porch with the two of them as they finished off the last of my candy bars. The rain was coming down harder and they decided they'd wait a few minutes to see if it let up. "We'll just hang out here, if that's all right," Ivory said, taking a seat on one of the dry patches of concrete and motioning for the cowboy to follow.

"Digger lives two streets away from yours, and we just thought we'd go through his neighborhood this year," Ivory explained as she carefully unwrapped a chocolate bar and stuffed the wrapper into one of the green knitted gloves she'd been wearing. "Last year, we collected donations for Save the Children in my neighborhood. But Digger's a big environmentalist, so this year it was Greenpeace."

"Tree hugger." Digger grinned through a mouthful of chocolate and caramel. "That's me."

While the rain drummed down on the metal roof over our heads, Ivory started going into a long explanation of the different causes Greenpeace helped: whales, rain forests, global warming. I brought up the topic of Digger's dog collar in the middle of global warming. It was the only thing I could think of to change the subject. Like "dog col-lar" was written in big letters across my brain or some-thing. "So what's up with that collar you wear around at school?" I said, reaching for the Snickers bag.

Digger shrugged. "It's different. Nobody else has one, right?"

Note to Digger: Maybe there's a good reason for that.

"Artistic expression," Ivory added. "He's an artist."

"You aren't wearing one tonight," I pointed out, and Ivory explained she and Digger had decided to be oppo-sites of themselves for Halloween. "This year, we wanted to be something we would never, in a million years, be in real life—so we picked a cheerleader and a cowboy."

"Yeah, can you see me sitting on a horse?" Digger said, grinning. "If I got up on one, in ten minutes it would be totally flat." He made a sound like air going out of a balloon (or somebody farting). "There goes Digger on his flat horse." Which made us almost fall off the porch laughing. Really.

"You're not that fat," I heard myself say when the laughter had died down a little.

Note to self: Are you blind? Why do you keep saying such dumb things?

"Right." Digger snorted as he crumpled up his candy wrappers and stuffed them into his jeans pocket. "I'm the poster child for fat."

After that, there was an uncomfortable silence when

nobody said anything. The rain on the porch roof suddenly seemed extra loud. Anybody passing by on the street must have done a double take at the three of us scrunched together, knee to knee, on the small square of dry land in the middle of the concrete. Now playing on Jerry Denny's porch: *Elvis, the Cheerleader, and the Cowboy.*

"Anybody seen any good movies lately?" Digger finally blurted out, which made everybody relax again.

Ivory asked me how my grandma was doing, if she was getting better. I told them how she was out of the hospital but in a physical therapy center. My mom had just sent me the new address, adding in capital letters how much my grandma would LOVE to hear from me. But my mom had no idea how crazy my life had been in Chicago. What would I write about? The Aloha jumpsuit? Viv? My dad storming out of the house that night?

Surprisingly, Ivory didn't ask anything about my dad until she and Digger were about to leave—which was unusual, considering what Ivory was normally like. We were standing around at the bottom of the porch steps. It had stopped raining briefly, and Ivory wanted to get back to Digger's house before it started to pour again, so his mom could drive her home.

"Did you say anything to your dad?" she asked in a low voice after Digger had moved a step or two away to call his mom on his cell phone. I appreciated the fact that Ivory wasn't spilling my whole life story in front of Digger, but it was still embarrassing.

I told her I'd talked to my dad that night.

"How'd he react?" she asked.

"Not great," I mumbled.

"Really?"

"Kind of," I said, not wanting to go through all the details of what had gone wrong. I could tell Ivory was already putting two and two together herself anyway.

"I'll try and figure out what you can do next." Ivory reached down to pick up her silver-and-green pom-poms from the steps. "But this is a good start, Josh." She shook one of her pom-poms in my direction.

"What's a good start?"

"Talking to him. And wearing his Elvis costume for Halloween, too."

Note to Ivory: The costume wasn't exactly my dad's idea.

"You look crazy but cool." She laughed. "I never thought you'd wear anything Elvis." Turning toward Digger, she added loudly, "Don't you agree?"

"Sure, right." Digger shoved his phone in his pocket and tried to act as if he hadn't been listening to our conversation the whole time.

"There's hope for you yet, Josh. That's what your horoscope said this week. Peace," Ivory finished.

She and Digger flashed me a peace sign and then the two of them went running—okay, with Digger, maybe "lumbering" is a better word—into the darkness. I could hear them chasing each other and laughing halfway down the street.

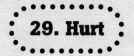

29. Hurt

Ivory may have believed there was hope for me. But my dad didn't. That was pretty clear. We didn't talk to each other again until supper the next night. After about fifteen minutes filled with nothing but the sound of our silverware clattering on our plates and the clock on the stove ticking, my dad finally cleared his throat and said, "Could you explain a few things to me, Josh?"

No, I couldn't.

But my dad continued without waiting for my answer. "This letter you sent"—he pushed the letter across the table toward me—"everything in it was made up?" He ran his finger along the words at the top. "There's no Chicago Elvis competition in the Grand Ballroom—or anywhere else?"

"No, not really—"

"Not really?"

"No, there isn't." The words stumbled stupidly out of my mouth.

"And the Las Vegas part was made up, too? There's no trip to Las Vegas for Elvis impersonators? There's no five-thousand-dollar prize? Anywhere?" Just by the tone of my dad's voice, I could tell he desperately wanted something, anything, to be true about my letter. Only there wasn't. Not one speck of truth. That's what made it worse.

I tried telling him I'd repay him for what he'd spent on the Aloha costume, even though I had no idea how I would actually do that. *Mow lawns until I was eighty?* I also said if he wanted to go ahead and perform at my school, I would understand. "I'll just deal with it," I told him. "You can call the music guy back if you want to."

My dad sighed loudly and pushed his chair away from the table. "It's not about the daggone costume or the dag-gone show, Josh." His silverware and dishes banged together loudly as he dumped them into the sink. "For cripes sake, I can get rid of the costume if I want to." My dad's voice rose. "I can sell it in the classifieds. Or put it in Viv's store. It's not about the costume or the letter or any of that other stuff, Josh. That's what you're not seeing. What really bothers me, what really hurt me about what happened yesterday, is what it shows about you and me," he said angrily, and stalked out of the room.

If I could be you,
if you could be me
for just one hour . . .
—"Walk a Mile in My Shoes," 1970

30. Why Tell Elvis Everything?

A few days later, I found a message from Ivory stuck to my locker. When I first saw the note as I came out of math class and glanced down the hall, my heart started hammering nervously. Who had left it there? What had they written? Of course, once I got closer, I could see the familiar scrawling letters in orange marker and the smiley face, which could only have come from—who else?

I tugged the note off the locker and read it:

> I have an idea about your dad. Stop by my locker at the end of school.

Ivory was the only person who'd been able to tell me anything about my dad. For the most part, Dad and I had still been avoiding each other. We went out of our way not to end up watching TV together in the living room or eating dinner at the same time. I made excuses about being too busy with homework or not being hungry at dinner-time. My dad stayed in his bedroom with the door closed, practicing and watching tapes of his shows.

But Ivory knew a lot more of the details because of her mom. It was like being in a giant game of Telephone, where the message is passed from one person to the next. My dad poured out his feelings to Viv, who told some things to Ivory, who passed them along to me.

Note to Dad: Do you know Viv is not very good at keeping secrets?

The day before, Ivory had told me my dad was trying to decide if he should quit being Elvis. "He had a long talk with my mom last night about looking for a new job," she said before classes started. "They made a lot of lists together."

"Lists?"

"Pros and cons. Being Elvis versus not being Elvis," Ivory continued. Then she dropped the bombshell that my dad was considering calling a therapist.

"What?" I said, loud enough for two kids in the hall to glance over at us.

"He told my mom he wants to work on improving your relationship with each other. He feels like he's been a bad father to you over the years, living so far away and everything."

I told Ivory the *last* thing I wanted to do was sit around in some therapist's office talking about my innermost feelings with my dad. "Can't you do something?"

Ivory said she'd try to get the message across to her mom. And if the Telephone game was working right, hopefully her mom would pass the word along to my dad, who would drop the whole idea.

"But we still need to come up with a way to get both of you to *talk* to each other at least. I mean, he's your dad, right? You can't keep being here . . . and there." She spread her arms out as if to demonstrate how far apart we were. I didn't bother to tell Ivory that we had always been that far apart. With about four states between us. I was used to it.

After getting Ivory's note about my dad, I waited for her at the end of the day. Just in case any of the vending machine guys happened to pass by, I stayed across the hall and pretended to be studying a row of old photographs showing Lister sports players from the 1950s (who all seemed to bear a vague resemblance to Elvis).

"Hey." Ivory bumped my back with her armful of books. Her hair was in two long braids and she was wearing a blouse that looked like it had come from an old *Brady Bunch* episode. Pink, white, and brown zigzag stripes. Like spumoni with a headache. "Why are you standing over here?"

"I'm trying to find a picture of someone I know."

Ivory rolled her eyes. "Right." She nodded toward her locker. "So come over here while I unload my stuff and I'll tell you my great idea." Keeping an eye on the hallway, I waited while Ivory put her books away. Other girls had mirrors and message boards and pictures in their lockers. Ivory had an embarrassing collection of stick-on stars and glow-in-the-dark planets.

"Okay," she said, tugging a large jeans purse over her shoulder and slamming the door shut on her mini universe. "Before I tell you my idea, you have to promise you'll do something to help me."

With Ivory, this could be a very dangerous promise to make, but I was getting desperate. I needed somebody (besides a therapist . . . *jeesh*) to give me some good advice for dealing with my dad. Or at least a plan for getting out of the mess I was in.

"Okay," I told Ivory cautiously. "What is it?"

"I want you to help Digger win in gym class."

"Win?"

"Hit a home run, or catch a ball." Ivory gestured at the air. "Something like that."

"We're playing volleyball. It doesn't have home runs."

Ivory glared at me. "You can think of something to let him win."

"I'm serious. He's really hopeless in gym."

"Do you want my help with your dad or not?"

I told Ivory I couldn't make any promises. "I'll try," I said.

"All right, here's my idea for your dad." Ivory dug around in her large purse. She pulled out a skinny blue ticket and held it toward me. In black type were these words: Jerry Denny as the King. Friday, November 12, at 8 p.m. Sponsored by the Winona Lions Club. Tickets: $15 at the door. $10 in advance.

I had to read it twice to realize that the ticket was referring to my dad. Jerry Denny. As the King.

"We're going to see one of his shows next week," Ivory said proudly, pushing the ticket into my hand. "Isn't that a brilliant idea?"

No, I wanted to say, *it isn't.* Because I didn't see how going to one of my dad's shows would change anything, other than making him really angry with me for showing up and upsetting him in front of a live audience. "How's this going to help?" I said, shoving the ticket into my back pocket.

Ivory didn't answer. She just kept babbling on about the show. "The tickets are already paid for and not returnable. My mom got them for us, so we can all go and see him. And besides, it's for a good cause. To raise money to help kids in hospitals. My mom will pick you up."

"Does my dad know anything about this?"

204

Ivory squinted at me as if I was the world's biggest moron. "Of course not, that's part of the surprise. He won't know we're there until he sees us in the audience."

"And what are we supposed to do then?"

"I don't know." Ivory's voice rose impatiently as she began to head down the hallway without waiting for me. "What do you usually do at concerts? Clap. Tell him it was great. Whatever you want to do."

"What if it's terrible?"

Spumoni Shirt didn't even turn to answer that question.

31. Hit or Miss

As it turned out, I wasn't the only person who got tickets from Ivory and her mom.

"I'm going to see Elvis," Gladys chirped the minute I stepped into her house.

I had stopped by to visit her on my way home from school on Friday. It had been a day or two since we had checked on her, so I thought I'd see how she was doing and say hello. When she told me she was going to see Elvis, I figured maybe she was a little mixed up about my dad or confused about something else. She often seemed to be lost in the past these days. But her eyes were bright and she did a shuffling dance in her pink rose slippers after she told me the news.

"Elvis?" I repeated.

Gladys reached for an envelope sitting on the doily-covered table by her front door and pulled out the same type of blue ticket Ivory had given me. I know I must have looked completely shocked. Like mouth-open, eyes-bugged-out shocked.

"You probably don't know the Mahoneys," Gladys began slowly, "but Vivian runs a little clothing store in town. Years ago, right after my husband died, I used to help out in her store on the weekends and do little sewing projects and clothing alterations for them. Just for my milk and bread money." Gladys gave a small laugh. "I can't do that kind of thing anymore, of course, but Vivian and her daughter still come by every once in a while to check up on me because I'm so"—her voice dropped to a whisper—"old. When they came by to visit yesterday, they brought me this ticket to see Elvis. Imagine that!" She waved the ticket in the air again.

In the game of Solitaire, this would have been the moment when a column of cards suddenly fit together, from the king at the top to the lowest card at the bottom. As Gladys talked, I remembered Ivory's story about the retired lady who'd helped out in their store. The one who had played "Chopsticks" on the piano when they had no customers. The one who had suggested the name Ivory.

That lady must have been Gladys.

And so Viv was the person who had introduced Gladys to my dad when he was looking for someone to sew his Elvis scarves. The whole time, of course, I had been under the impression that Gladys was just a lonely old lady living all by herself, but now it seemed Ivory and Viv (and probably half of Chicago) had been keeping her company, too.

"The two of them were nice enough to give me this for free." Gladys held the ticket toward me. "Look at that. It cost ten dollars—my stars, can you believe it? Why, when I saw Elvis at the Chicago Amphitheater in 1957, it was only a dollar or two."

"You saw the real Elvis?" This was getting more and more bizarre.

Gladys nodded. "He was gold—all gold. I'll never forget it. He looked like"—she closed her eyes as if she was trying to picture the scene again—"a king, or a movie star . . . or somebody like that."

A gold Elvis?

"His suit was gold lamé," Gladys explained. (Which didn't really clear things up for me.) "And now, all these years later, I'm going to see him again. Who would have guessed that?" She did her shuffle dance on the carpet again. "I'll have to try and behave myself, won't I?"

In my opinion, the whole plan had disaster written all over it. My dad didn't know we were coming. Gladys didn't know she was going to see Jerry Denny instead of solid-gold Elvis. And as if that wasn't bad enough, I found out Digger was coming along, too. Ivory called to tell me she had invited him to be her date. That's what she told me—her *date. Jeesh.* I didn't even want to visualize that.

"Remember what you said about helping Digger in gym class," Ivory reminded me on a daily basis as the day of the show approached.

Watching how badly Digger played volleyball, I believed it would probably be easier to turn my dad into Elvis—the *real* Elvis—than to turn Digger into a good volleyball player. Every single one of his serves nailed the net. If he was on your team, you could forget about making any points. He would completely miss the ball or smack it foul every single time. I had no clue how I was going to help him win anything.

My chance finally came on a day when Digger and I were on opposite sides. Dave Ernst was my captain and we had a pretty good team, but we were losing by two points when I moved up to the front. "Comeback time," Dave yelled from the back, where he was serving for our team.

Of course Dave served the ball straight at Digger, who was in the middle of the second row on the other side of the net. Easy point, right? However, by some kind of divine intervention, Digger actually hit the ball. It soared back over the net toward me. As my hands reached up to smack the ball, my head remembered my promise to

Ivory—so as my hands were going for the ball, my brain was screaming that I should let it go. *Hit it. Let it go. Hit it. . . .* In the middle of this complete brain freeze, the ball dropped to the gym floor.

While Digger's team cheered and pounded him on the back, Dave stared at me in total disbelief. His arms pumped up and down in the air. "What were you doing?" he shouted. Even though it was only one missed hit, we ended up losing the game after the other team got the ball back and scored the winning points.

I don't know what winning the game did for Digger, but I know what losing it did for me. It cost me a bag of chips and one can of soda at lunch because Dave said he wanted payback for my boneheaded play in gym. "You owe me," he said, smacking the back of my head as he walked past me at lunchtime. "I'll take some chips and a Pepsi."

The rest of the week, I had to put up with being barked at every time I sat down for lunch. I'd get to the table and the other guys would start barking and goofing around. "Don't hit the ball at me, Dog Face," they'd say, pretending to flail wildly at an invisible ball in the air.

It kind of surprised me to get treated like that. *Over one stupid play.* A play that I could have made with my eyes closed if I hadn't been holding up my end of the deal with Ivory. In the back of my mind, I wondered if maybe that had been Ivory's real plan all along. Maybe it hadn't been about Digger at all. Maybe she'd been hoping to turn Dave Ernst and the vending machine guys against me. Maybe she was under the delusion that I'd come over and join her table if it worked? Right.

The whole experience reminded me of the afternoon when Gladys and I had played Go Fish and trying to lose had been a lot harder than trying to win.

32. Rhinestone Sneakers

On the day of the show, Ivory left another note on my locker:

Tonight, 6 p.m. Be ready.

I was having second thoughts about the whole idea. My dad had been arguing with me all week about everything—from how much television I was watching to who was supposed to answer the phone when it rang.

Note to Dad: Why is it my job to answer your Elvis calls?

Even ordering pizza was an argument. "Can't you just pick up the phone and order something for us for dinner, Josh?" my dad had snapped at me the night before. "You're thirteen years old, for cripes sake. I've got one day left to get ready for the big show I'm doing this week. Can't you just do one daggone thing to help me out?" He yanked the headphones off his head and threw them on his bed before making the phone call himself.

After that, I called Ivory and told her the idea wasn't going to work.

"Of course it will," she insisted.

"He's being a complete jerk."

"He told my mom you're being a complete jerk," Ivory retorted.

"Who do you believe?"

Ivory was silent for a minute. "Both of you."

I told Ivory I might decide at the last minute to stay home. "I'm not promising anything. If he keeps being a jerk, I'm not going. I'll just give you the ten bucks back for the ticket." Ivory said Gladys would be very disappointed if we didn't see the show.

"Then take her and go."

But Ivory insisted they weren't going without me.

On the night of the show, the doorbell rang an hour earlier than it was supposed to ring. I glanced at the clock. It was only five. My dad had left in such a panicked rush, with clothes draped over his shoulder and equipment piled up in his arms, I figured he was probably back because he had forgotten something.

But when I opened the door, I found Gladys standing on our porch. "I know I'm early," she said in an apologetic

213

voice. "But I wanted to be sure not to miss my ride to the show. You know how forgetful us old ladies can be sometimes." She tapped her head. "Nothing much upstairs these days."

She looked like a walking jewelry box. Huge gold-and-pearl earrings were clipped to her ears. Two pearl necklaces dangled around her neck and a large silver piano was pinned to her bright red coat. "How do I look?" she said, patting her curly white hair and turning around in a little circle once she stepped inside. I tried not to stare at her shoes, which were gold sneakers decorated with red rhinestones.

"You look nice," I said uncomfortably.

"I even got my nails done for Elvis." She held out her painted nails for me to see. I could tell she was proud of how she looked, but all I could think about was the fact that I was going to be walking around with her.

Of course, Ivory and her mom thought Gladys looked gorgeous. Those were their words when they picked us up. "Look at those gorgeous earrings and your cute shoes, Gladys." Ivory had on her rainbow beret and the same hippie outfit she'd been wearing on the first day I'd met her. Digger was wearing his usual dog collar and a black ELVIS LIVES T-shirt. The extra large Elvis face seemed to float in the middle of his chest like some kind of strange apparition. The three of us crowded into the backseat of Viv's car, carrying our winter coats. Gladys sat in the front.

"Everybody ready to go and meet Elvis?" Ivory's mom said in her Viv's Vintage voice, and we headed for the show.

By the time we finally stopped, my right leg was asleep and my hands were so sweaty I had to keep rubbing them on my jeans to dry them off. The show was in a small town called Winona, which was a lot farther away than Ivory had told me.

When we pulled into the parking lot and got out of the car, the air didn't even smell like Chicago anymore. It smelled like fields and farms and cows. And I guess everybody in town must have decided seeing Elvis was better than sitting around Winona doing nothing, because the parking lot was packed with pickup trucks and big, shiny cars. Viv got one of the last open spots.

As we walked to the old theater where the show was being held, I looked up at the glaring sign that announced TONIGHT! WINONA LIONS CLUB WELCOMES JERRY DENNY AS ELVIS. My stomach began to do nervous flip-flops. A long line of people, bundled up in their winter coats, trailed out the doors of the building. All of these people who didn't even know Jerry Denny had come to see him pretend to be Elvis? It was kind of frightening.

"Hey," Digger said loudly, bumping my arm. "Your dad must be pretty good. Look at the big line."

I spun around. "Stop talking about him, okay?" The last thing I needed was for a hundred strangers standing in line to find out that the JERRY DENNY in big glowing letters on the theater sign was my dad.

Ivory and Digger exchanged glances and Digger shut up. Behind us, Viv and Gladys made their way slowly across the parking lot, arm in arm, reminding me of my mom and grandma walking together. Gladys kept saying, "My, it's cold tonight, isn't it?" As we got into line, I could feel people's eyes glancing at us. (Okay, looking mainly at Digger's dog collar and Ivory's beret and Gladys's rhinestone shoes.) They were probably wondering what part of Winona we were from.

At the ticket window, two white-haired old men were taking the tickets. They tore each one in half with their trembling hands and then handed them back through the window, saying things like, "Enjoy the show" and "Hope you brought your blue suede shoes." They seemed to know most of the people in line by name, which was why the line was moving so slowly, I think. When they got to us, one of the men asked, "Where you folks from?" Viv said we had driven from Chicago. Thankfully, she didn't add that we were good friends with Elvis. The man smiled and handed the ticket stubs back. "Come back and see us again sometime."

Not very likely.

The theater had about twenty rows of seats with a small stage at the front. Most of the seats were already full when we walked in, except for an empty section in the middle of the fifth row, which turned out to be ours. As we squeezed past the other people in our row, I could feel my heart hammering. Why did our seats have to be so close? And right in the middle? There was no means of escape, except by climbing over the laps of about eight large strangers.

Gladys and Viv sat on one side of me, and Digger was on the other side, with Ivory next to him. The old wooden seats were the kind that squeak when you push them down. Mine had a missing armrest and somebody had carved their initials inside a heart on the curved wooden back.

"Isn't this place wonderful?" Gladys whispered, and patted my arm. "Look how close we are to the stage, Josh. Elvis is going to be right up there in front, isn't he?"

"Probably." I slouched farther down in my chair, taking the chance the entire thing might fold up with me inside it.

Ivory passed a box of Sno-Caps down the row. "Want some?" she said, reaching around Digger, who was ignoring me. I shook my head and Ivory gave me one of her "what the heck is up with you" looks before she poured the rest of the box into Digger's hand.

It seemed like forever before somebody finally came onstage to announce that the show was about to start. A tall, bearded man with a cowboy hat and boots (reminiscent of Digger's Halloween costume) stepped out through the stage curtains to thank us for coming out and supporting the Winona Lions Club. "We've got a real treat for all you folks out there in Winona tonight," he said, leaning over the microphone, which was too short for him. "All the way from the bright lights of the big city, please welcome Chicago's own Jerry Denny as Elvis Presley!"

And then the lights went out and this *Star Wars*–type music started playing. Really, you would have expected the *Millennium Falcon* to come rising up from the stage at any moment. Slowly and agonizingly, the red curtains jerked open little by little, but the stage was empty and dark. There was no Jerry Denny or Elvis standing there. *Oh god.* My hands reached up to cover my eyes because I didn't want to watch the whole disaster unfold. A few people around us snickered.

A spotlight came on and moved back and forth across the empty stage, as if it couldn't find the performer, either. Little bits of dust swirled like mini tornadoes in the light. Suddenly a voice said dramatically over the loudspeaker, "Ladies and gentlemen, please put your hands together for Jerry Denny as the King."

My head pounded—*blam, blam, blam*—and I felt like I

couldn't breathe. I slid lower in the seat, hoping it would swallow me up in its creaky wooden jaws. And then the spotlight caught a white jumpsuit moving quickly across the stage. The audience began clapping and shouting, "Elvis, Elvis. . . ."

Gladys's fingers tightened excitedly on my arm. "It's him," she whispered. "It's Elvis."

33. Jerry Denny as the King

Really, I could have believed it was Elvis, because the person standing onstage looked nothing like Jerry Denny. I stared at the figure posed like a statue in the spotlight, with his legs slightly apart, microphone at his lips, left arm pointing at an angle. I hardly recognized my own dad. Somehow on the stage, he seemed taller. And younger. In the spotlight, the Aloha Eagle costume looked like the real thing, not just white polyester and fake glass stones.

"Well, it's one for the money." Elvis began to move.

"Two for the show." His arm dropped and his head snapped to the other side. "Three to get ready." He spun the other way. "Now go, cat, go...." Elvis's heel began bouncing up and down, and pretty soon his whole leg was shaking by itself. As he danced across the stage strumming his guitar, the audience whistled and clapped. Blue and red rhinestone eagles sparkled in the stage lights. The gold stars on his jumpsuit shone as he leaned toward the front row, snapping his fingers and singing about nobody stepping on his blue suede shoes.

I don't think I breathed during the entire song. Next to me, Gladys clapped her hands and Digger's leg bounced up and down in time to the music. But I sat frozen in my chair, as if one wrong move might break the whole spell. As if Elvis might glance out into the audience, see me, and in a flash of smoke turn back into Jerry Denny, divorced dad and out-of-work shoe salesman.

When the song finished, somebody behind us shouted, "We love you, Elvis!"

My dad shaded his eyes against the spotlights. "Thank you, honey. I can't see nothin' up here, but I love you, too." That's when I began to realize that it wasn't just my dad who was pretending to be Elvis. Everybody in the audience was pretending, too. The people around us weren't sitting in a dusty old theater in Winona, Illinois, watching a forty-year-old guy from Chicago sing like Elvis. They were picturing themselves somewhere else, watching the real Elvis, the King himself.

Even when Elvis's belt fell off, people kept right on pretending. In the middle of the song "Suspicious Minds," when my dad was doing a knee-bending, arm-swinging move, the big gold eagle belt of his Aloha jumpsuit just popped right off and thumped onto the stage. But the music kept right on playing, and Elvis kept singing, and at the end of the song my dad calmly picked up his belt, fastened it back on, and said in his fake Southern drawl, "Well now, folks, sure hope nothin' else falls off tonight." The whole audience cracked up.

Later on, my dad came out with an armful of Gladys's scarves for the song "Love Me Tender." I guess everybody in Winona must have known about this Elvis tradition, because people started lining up the minute they spotted them. You would have thought he was handing out hundred-dollar bills. There were old ladies, moms with little kids, and even one or two teenagers. The scarf line stretched way past our row. Each time my dad draped one of those scarves over some lady's shoulders, she got this look on her face like he had just put a wreath of roses around her neck. Or like someone had just told her, *I pronounce you Queen*. It was bizarre.

Viv and Gladys got in line with everybody else, and you could tell my dad was surprised to see them when they reached the front of the stage. As he looked down, his voice wavered a little in the song and a smile crept across his face, although I don't think anybody noticed it except us. Reaching out, he kissed Viv's hand before he put a bright yellow scarf around her neck. And then (this was kind of surprising) he bent down on one knee and sang the last line of "Love Me Tender" to eighty-seven-year-old Gladys. "For, my darlin', I love you, and I always will. . . ."

After he finished singing, my dad draped a lavender scarf around Gladys's neck and leaned down to kiss her paper-white cheek. The entire audience clapped. Really, it was a pretty touching moment (and I'm a guy). When she got back to her seat, Gladys's eyes were still bright and sparkling. "If I wasn't so old," she whispered to me, "I'd marry Elvis in a minute."

My dad spotted me during that part of the show, I think. He must have seen Gladys and Viv come back to our row and noticed me sitting beside Digger and Ivory. But I didn't realize he knew I was in the crowd until the song "Teddy Bear." He was tossing teddy bears into the audience (apparently this was an Elvis tradition, too). Looking across the theater, he gave a little wave at me and sent a bear flying over five rows of people. As I reached up and caught it, I suddenly had this weird feeling of being five years old again—when little things like getting a stuffed animal from my dad used to make me happy.

Oh let me be
your Teddy Bear.
—"(Let Me Be Your) Teddy
Bear," 1957

34. Such a Night

The audience didn't want the show to end. Maybe because Winona isn't the kind of place where much happens, people stayed in their seats and kept on clapping and clapping after the curtain slid closed. My dad finally came out to do an encore. You could tell he wasn't used to doing encores very often, because he couldn't find his way out of the stage curtains—all you could see was his hand pushing and tugging on the red velvet drapes for a minute or two.

When he finally did find an opening to slip through, he had to tell the sound guy which track to play. "Number five, Joe," he said, holding up five fingers. Then he turned toward the audience and wiped the perspiration off his face with a long blue scarf. "Everybody ready to rock?" he shouted into the microphone. The crowd roared. "Well then let's all stand up and dance to this last number."

You could hear a whooshing groan echoing through the whole theater as people got up from their wooden seats. But when "Jailhouse Rock" began playing, everybody started swaying and bobbing their heads to the music. Some women—like the very wide ones in front of me—even tried twisting their hips. Winona, Illinois, became one big cell block dancing to the Jailhouse Rock . . .

I'm embarrassed to admit I stood up with everybody else. Ivory, Digger, and I pretended we were playing a huge piano. Leaning from left to right, we moved our hands back and forth along the seats in front of us as if they were a big keyboard. When I thought about it later, I couldn't believe I acted like such a geek. What thirteen-year-old from Boston dances to "Jailhouse Rock"? What had happened to me in Chicago?

It was easy to get pulled into the illusion even after the show ended. We watched people posing for pictures with my dad and getting autographs in the theater lobby after he finished. They would walk away, waving his signature in the air proudly, as if it was the real thing. As if it said Elvis Presley, not Jerry Denny.

I could feel people turning to stare at the six of us when we left, too. I swear you could almost hear them whispering, *Look, it's the King and his family* as we walked out beside my dad in his rhinestone-sparkling jumpsuit. It made me feel like turning and waving, the way movie stars do when they stroll down the red carpet to their limos.

Once we got outside, my dad couldn't stop talking. His voice was loud and excited as we stood by Viv's car in the parking lot. "So what'd you think? Wasn't that a great crowd tonight?" His hands gestured in the air. "I mean, I felt like they were really with me tonight. They were with me, weren't they?"

You could tell he was still in Elvis land and didn't even notice the cold. It had started to snow and, weirdly, even the falling snow kind of looked like rhinestones as it sparkled in the parking lot lights. My dad's voice rolled on, throwing out question after question—and then answering most of them without even waiting for us. "How was my voice tonight, Viv? I've been working hard on the voice all week. I thought the voice was on tonight. It was, wasn't it? You know"—he ruffled his Elvis hair—"I can't come up with a single thing that went wrong. The voice, the moves, it was all working tonight. Man, Elvis would have been proud of me tonight, wouldn't he? I think he would've been proud."

He draped his arm over my shoulders. "And then to have my son here and my friends and my favorite neighbor, Gladys"—he broke into a wide smile—"I mean, what a night, as Elvis would say!"

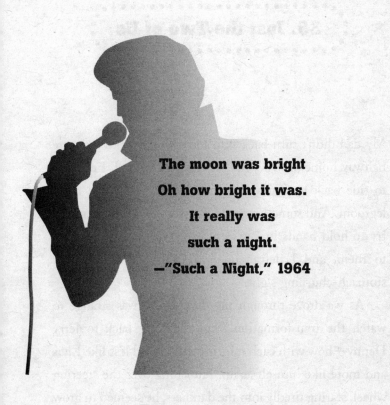

The moon was bright
Oh how bright it was.
It really was
such a night.
—"Such a Night," 1964

35. Just the Two of Us

My dad didn't turn back into Jerry Denny until we were halfway home. Since Viv's car was so crowded, I decided to ride back to Chicago with him. At least I had more legroom. And something told me Ivory and Digger might try to hold hands in Viv's car, even with me sitting next to them, and I definitely didn't want to witness that stomach-churning sight.

As we drove through the darkness, it was strange to watch the transformation from the King back to Jerry Denny—how with each mile my dad looked less like Elvis and more like himself again. Hunching over the steering wheel, staring tiredly into the darkness, he seemed to grow quieter and smaller the farther away we got. "Hand me one of those throat lozenges," he said after a while, point-ing toward the glove box. "My throat is killing me." The sharp smell of lemon filled the car as he crunched them loudly between his teeth (which is a habit of his that drives me crazy).

Elvis was definitely gone.

"So. . . ." He cleared his throat after nobody had said anything for a few miles. "I know we haven't been getting along very well these last couple of weeks, and I wanted to talk about some things with you."

Great. I sunk deeper into my coat. This was what I had been afraid of when I'd agreed to ride back with him. That once he had me trapped in his car in the middle of nowhere, he would try to have his serious dad-to-son talk with me.

"You know why I like being Elvis?" he asked, glancing over at me. When I didn't answer right away, he said, "Because it lets me be somebody different than who I usually am. You know what I mean? When you're Elvis, people notice you. You're important for a little while. People don't look at you the same way they did before." He shifted in his seat. "Don't get me wrong, I know I'm not Elvis. Nobody can be Elvis—the real Elvis. Elvis was Elvis. There'll never be another person like him. But when I'm up there onstage, pretending to be him, wearing his outfits and singing his music, I'm a different person. I can make people laugh and smile and kiss their girlfriends and fall in love again—"

"Dad, jeez." I gave him a look.

He kept talking. "For years I've been trying to figure out who Jerry Denny is and what he's good at doing. I know I drove your mom crazy sometimes. There were days when I was working in the shoe store, listening to people talk about their ingrown toenails and their foot fungus, when I would think to myself—what in the heck am I doing here?"

His eyes glanced at me again. "I know I've gotta understand where you're coming from, too. That's what Viv says. You're thirteen and you just want to fit in. You don't want a nutcase for a dad." He reached for another throat lozenge and popped it in his mouth. "Heck, when I was thirteen," he said, crunching loudly, "I remember being completely humiliated by my dad's grease-stained hands. He was a mechanic and I never wanted him to pick me up after school because I didn't want my friends to see those hands and know what he did for a living." My dad laughed.

"So I understand why you sent that letter." His voice grew more serious. "Don't get me wrong, it upset me at the time—it got my hopes up about going to Vegas and everything—but that wasn't all your fault. It was partly mine for not seeing how you felt about what I was doing and how it was messing up things for you at school.

"I'm gonna make it a goal to tone down the Elvis stuff the rest of the time you're here. And I'm gonna try to pay more attention to you and not be so caught up in it all."

He thumped his hands down on the steering wheel for emphasis. "So that's my speech. Not another word. Have I put you to sleep?"

"No," I mumbled. Trying to figure out what I was supposed to say next, I added kind of awkwardly, "The show was good tonight. People really liked it."

"Yeah, it was a good crowd," my dad replied. "I had fun."

I know there were a lot of other things I should have said—how I was sorry, how he was way better as Elvis than I had imagined, how I'd go to another show if he wanted me to—but that was the best I could do right then. There's only so much you can say when you're sitting next to your dad in a car, just the two of you, driving through the dark and the snow in the middle of Illinois.

It was one o'clock in the morning when we finally pulled into the driveway of my dad's house. After we got inside, he went around turning on all the lights as if he wasn't planning on going to bed anytime soon. "I don't know about you, but I'm starving," he said, tossing his coat on the living room couch. "You know what Elvis would say? A nice fried peanut butter and banana sandwich would taste just great right now." He rubbed his hands together. "I'm gonna change out of my costume and then we'll start cooking."

We stayed up for another hour making sandwiches in the kitchen. While the rest of the world was snoring away, we were slathering butter on slices of white bread, adding large quantities of peanut butter and mashed bananas in the middle, and frying them to a nice golden brown. (Okay, so we burned one side of them, but that was not my fault.)

When they were done, we ate them straight out of the pan. "No plates for real men," my dad said. So we sat on the countertop and ate the sandwiches with our fingers. Blobs of banana ended up on our shirts and the floor. We were even wiping banana off our socks at one point. It was pretty humorous.

Maybe because he was so full of carbs and sugar, Dad started talking about Viv and how much he liked her. "I know she's different," he said through a thick mouthful of peanut butter. "With that reddish hair and all that makeup. Do you know she has a tattoo?"

Note to Dad: I don't really want to know, to tell you the truth.

"Yep. She's got a big daisy tattooed on her shoulder. I mean it's this big." He pointed to his palm. "Your mom would die if she knew—God, she would just die." He shook his head. "But Viv's got a good heart and she's a hard worker. That business of hers makes nothing, I'm telling you, but somehow she keeps it together. She's a

234

good person inside." He looked at me anxiously. "Do you like her so far from what you've seen?"

I shrugged. "Sure, she's nice, I guess." Which was the most I was ever going to say about anybody who wasn't my mom. I didn't feel like I knew that much about Viv yet—not enough to have an opinion at least. She was a good driver. She was nice to Gladys. She had a weird store where nobody bought anything. That was about it.

My dad took another bite of sandwich and nodded. "You seem like you get along with her anyway."

It was a strange feeling to hang out in the kitchen with my dad at one o'clock in the morning, eating fried banana sandwiches and talking about his girlfriend. Strange, but good. Like I could see us doing this again as we got older: the two of us hanging out together in our old T-shirts and boxer shorts, sharing a pizza or whatever, and talking about guy stuff.

36. Separate Ways

One of the biggest problems with being a divorced kid is that the minute you get used to one place, one parent, one life—you get yanked back to the other. It's Murphy's Law for Divorced Kids. Just when you start thinking, *I could stay here,* it's time to pack up and leave. Which is why I shouldn't have been surprised when my mom called a week later to tell me it was time to head back to Boston.

The phone rang at ten on a Saturday morning. I'd been to another Elvis show with my dad the night before. (Well, not really a show, more of an off-key sing-along with a lot of senior citizens.) He'd performed at a place called Stonebridge Estates, which was like Shadyside Villas only with apartments instead of trailers. All my dad needed was for somebody to push a track button every time a new song was supposed to play, but he claimed this was an important job. "Would you mind coming along and giving me a hand with this gig?" he'd asked me. "I could really use the help."

At the end of the show, he introduced me to the audience as his new sound guy. "Didn't Josh do a great job tonight?" From the way the old people clapped, you would have thought I was directing Elvis's band instead of pushing a few buttons on a machine. The rest of the night, I couldn't get the songs out of my head. I could still hear the words to "Hound Dog" (track number two on my dad's playlist) in my sleep.

When the phone rang the next morning, my dad picked it up. I could tell it was my mom. As I was lying in bed, I heard Dad stumble down the steps from his bedroom to find the phone, which was probably stuck somewhere in the living room sofa. "Hello?" he shouted. And then, in a lower voice, "Sorry, couldn't find the phone." As he walked down the hallway toward my room, I could hear him curtly agreeing to whatever was being said. Everything was a short answer: "Good. Yes. Sure. I understand. No problem. Fine. I'll do that. I'll get him." By then I had already guessed what my mom was calling about.

My dad knocked softly on my door, as if he didn't want to wake me. I thought about just rolling over and pretending to be asleep.

The doorknob turned and Dad peeked in. "You awake?"

"Sure." I reached reluctantly for the phone and my dad slipped out of the room.

"Well, I'm finally calling with some good news," Mom chattered, in a voice that sounded breezy and relaxed for the first time in a long time. "Your grandma is doing much better and she's scheduled to come home sometime in the next few days."

Of course this was good news. I wanted my grandma to be okay again and for everything to go back to the way it used to be, right? The news at six-thirty. The walk-abouts. The card games.

"I've hired a nice lady to help her around the house, so if all goes well—fingers crossed—she'll be home by next weekend and we can be back in Boston sometime after Thanksgiving. Just in time to start decorating for Christmas," my mom joked. "I thought you'd be excited to hear the news. I know it's been a long time to be away from your friends."

While Mom kept talking, I tried to convince myself how great it was to be going home. In a week or two, I'd be back with Brian and the other guys. The basketball season would be starting. There would be folded socks in my drawers again (yes, my mom even folded the socks) and my dinners wouldn't come from either the microwave or the local takeout.

"Do you have a pencil and paper handy?" Mom asked. "I've got a list of things I don't want you to forget in Chicago."

But as she recited her list, my mind began to drift off. I started thinking about all the things I wouldn't forget in Chicago—fried peanut butter and banana sandwiches, for instance. Closely followed by: seeing my dad covered in black hair dye, the Elvis show in Winona, the home run I hit in gym class, Ivory's weird clothes—

"Are you writing this down?"

"Sure," I told my mom.

**Sometimes I want to stay here,
then again I want to leave . . .
then again I want to stay.
—"I Feel So Bad," 1961**

37. Elvisly Yours

On my last day at Listerine, my locker was plastered with blue and orange streamers and balloons and handwritten signs with the words GOOD LUCK, JOSH on them. When he saw the decorations, the guy next to me thought I had made it on the Listerine basketball team. "Congratulations," he said, chomping on a huge wad of gum and tugging his books out of his locker. I told him I wasn't on the team, I was moving back to Boston. His eyebrows rose. "Bummer."

The vending machine crowd hadn't been much different when I told them, either. Actually, I told Dave in gym class first. We were doing our stretches before class one morning and I said, "I'm gonna be moving back to Boston next week, so this is my last week at Listerine. I'm just trying to let everybody know."

Dave kept swinging his body in half circles—first to one side, then the other. "You flying?"

"Yeah."

"That's good" was all he said. I don't know what I expected Dave or anybody else to do. Guys aren't going to boo-hoo over you and tell you they'll miss you forever. But I guess I thought they'd at least take up a collection for an honorary bag of M&M's for me. You know, send one flying down the table: *This one's for Josh!* Or smack me on the back and say, *See you around, Boston dude.* But my last day at the vending machine table wasn't much different than my first one. I sat at the end of the table and the guy next to me drank his usual five cartons of milk. I caught two bags of snacks. And when the bell rang, everybody got up and left. The next week, some new home run hitter was probably sitting in my seat.

The locker decorations surprised me a little, though. I wasn't sure who would have done it until I noticed the little smiley faces, stars, and peace signs scattered around the edges of the signs. Later on, Ivory told me how she and Digger and a few of their friends had come in before school started to put up everything. "Did you see the ones that said ROCK ON, JOSH and DON'T GET ALL SHOOK UP?" Ivory asked, with a fake innocent look. "I put those up because I figured it doesn't matter if people know about Elvis now, right? I mean, you'll be a million miles away, so who cares?"

My dad invited Gladys, Viv, and Ivory (who brought along Digger, of course) to come over for a going-away lunch on the Saturday I was leaving. He ordered fried chicken and mashed potatoes from KFC, and Viv brought a home-made chocolate cheesecake. We ate on HAPPY BIRTHDAY paper plates in my dad's living room.

Even though my suitcases were sitting in the hallway, everybody tried to avoid talking about how I was leaving for Boston in a few hours. I don't think Gladys even real-ized I was going away. We were sitting next to each other on the couch with our plates balanced on our legs and she said, "What a nice birthday party this is, Josh. Thank you for inviting me."

"It isn't my birthday," I tried to tell her.

She looked up, confused. "Well, whose is it?"

"I'm going home to Boston."

"Oh, don't leave just yet," she said, reaching over and patting my hand. "The party's just getting started." In some ways, I felt like maybe Gladys was right.

"Time for opening gifts," my dad announced when we had run out of cheerful and upbeat things to keep talking about and when the food was gone.

"We'll start," Viv said as she reached for a square pack-age sitting next to her purse. "This is a gift from Ivory and me." She handed me a package wrapped in silver paper that I was fairly sure had been reused. Maybe everything in their lives was reused, who knows?

The gift turned out to be *A Year of Horoscopes and Sun*

Signs. Inside, they had written: Good luck in Boston, Josh. Elvisly Yours, Ivory and Viv.

"You'll be surprised at how often those forecasts are right," Ivory insisted. "It will change your life."

"Thanks. That's great." I politely paged through the book, even though I didn't plan on believing in the predictions of the stars and planets anytime soon.

"And this is just something small from me." Digger reached into his pocket and pulled out a crumpled package that had been taped together with masking tape. "Sorry for the bad wrap job," he said with a smile. Inside was a small brown leather band with shiny silver rivets and a snap fastener. I tried not to wonder if it was a dog collar for a poodle.

"It's to wear on your wrist," Digger said proudly. "I made it."

I was pretty surprised to find out that Digger actually *made* the pieces he wore. Even though Ivory had said Digger was an artist, I figured his collars and stuff had come straight from the local pet store. Not that he made them himself.

"He makes belts and wallets and all kinds of things," Viv explained to my dad and Gladys. "He's a very talented young man."

I fastened the band on my wrist. It wasn't something I'd ever wear under normal circumstances, but it was okay for the moment: for my dad's living room in Chicago anyway, for a going-away party. "Thanks," I said, glancing over at him.

Digger nodded. "No problem."

"Last present," my dad said as he leaned forward to hand me a small, flat package about the size of a deck of playing cards. I tore off the wrapping to find a blue silk scarf signed *Jerry Denny, your Elvis dad* in black marker.

"Gladys sewed the scarf and I signed it," my dad explained proudly. "We wanted you to have a little Elvis souvenir to take back to Boston with you."

Most of the people I knew in Boston, including my mom, would have no clue what it was. She still hadn't heard about my dad being Elvis. "I'll tell her when the time's right," my dad kept saying, but that hadn't happened yet. So the gift wasn't exactly something I could take back to Boston and hang up on my wall for everybody to see. But my dad didn't need to know all that. "Thanks," I said. "It's cool."

Reaching behind the couch, I pulled out the round, tissue-paper-wrapped package I'd been waiting to give to him. It had taken a lot of planning to get the gift from the window of Viv's Vintage to Ivory's house to mine. Ivory had brought it to school and I had kept it on the top shelf of my locker for a few days before smuggling it home in my backpack. "I've got one more present," I said, handing it to my dad, who gave me a surprised glance.

From the outside, the gift looked like a large white bowling ball because of all the tissue paper and tape I had used. As my dad began unwrapping the layers of paper, everybody leaned forward to catch the first glimpse of what was inside. Finally, after one last tug of paper and tape, it appeared: a plaster head with a chipped nose and rosy cheeks and black-painted sideburns.

"Elvis!" my dad shouted.

It was the perfect gift for him. Seriously, it was.

After the party, I left Chicago. It was snowing when the plane landed in Boston that night and everything looked different than when I'd left. Even the airport seemed strange, as if I had just landed in some foreign country where I didn't know a soul and where everything felt unfamiliar.

My mom met me at the Arrivals gate. She had gotten there an hour early, she said. "But it gave me time to make up my grocery list for next week." She held up a list written on the back of an envelope, and I had to admit it was kind of a relief to see my mom hadn't changed—except for having a completely sunburned face.

"I realized I'd been in Florida for almost four months and I had barely seen the sun because I'd been so busy with

Grandma," she explained. "So the day before I left, I sat outside in one of Grandma's lawn chairs with a magazine and fell asleep. Wasn't that a crazy thing to do?" She gave an embarrassed laugh.

Post-it note #5 on the dashboard: BUY SUNBURN CREAM.

Once we got in the car, it wasn't long before the whole story about Elvis and my dad came pouring out. I could hide things from my mom over the phone, but I couldn't hide them from her in person. It started with a comment about my sneakers, which weren't looking great after several months of being worn around Chicago—and hadn't looked good before that, either. "Your dad couldn't get you a deal on a pair of shoes while you were there?" Mom said, noticing them as soon as I stepped out of the snowy slush into the car.

"They're okay," I replied, trying to shove my feet farther under the dash.

"How's business going at the store?"

"I don't know." I shifted uncomfortably. "Dad's doing some new stuff now."

"New stuff? He isn't working at Murphy's anymore?" As she backed out of the airport parking space, my mom's eyes darted from the rearview mirror, to me, and back. "What's he doing instead?"

I could tell I was trapped. There was no good way to say it. At least none that I could think of. And really, how was I supposed to talk about living in Chicago without ever mentioning Elvis?

"He's doing some singing," I said. "As Elvis."

"What?" From my mom's shocked expression and tone, you would have thought I'd just told her my dad had shaved his head and become a Buddhist monk. "Elvis? With the jumpsuit and the sunglasses? That kind of Elvis?"

"He has his own singing business," I tried to explain. "Going around as Elvis."

Her voice was incredulous. "Your dad dresses up as Elvis?"

"Kind of, yeah."

"And people pay him to sing? That's his job now?"

"Yeah."

My mom shook her head. "I can't believe that. I really cannot believe that. . . ." She kept on shaking her head for about the next twenty-five miles. I don't think she got the idea at all. How my dad was just trying something different. How he wasn't the same old Jerry Denny she knew. How he was pretty good at being Elvis and how people actually lined up for his shows. But right then, as we were speeding along a Boston freeway, I didn't really feel like getting into some deep discussion about it. So I kept my mouth shut. Let Elvis stay in Chicago and my mom in Boston. Some things (like the divorce plants, for instance) couldn't be moved from one place to the other.

38. Viva Las Vegas

A few months after I left Chicago, Dad was invited to be Elvis for the spring dance at Listerine—which just goes to show you that life sometimes has a strange way of working out. Ivory told me the theme was "Jump Back to the Past." I guess he was asked to sing a few songs and pose for class photographs in his Aloha Eagle costume. According to Ivory, there were pictures of my dad everywhere after the dance—in the school newspaper and the yearbook and even taped up in kids' lockers.

Note: My dad's face with sideburns and sunglasses smiling inside everybody's locker at Charles W. Lister was something I didn't really want to imagine.

Dave Ernst was elected "King" of the dance by the seventh grade, so his picture was in the local paper. Ivory mailed a copy to me. The photo showed him standing next to my dad with the caption "Dance King Meets Real King." *Jeesh.*

My dad eventually got to Las Vegas, too—although he didn't get there by being Elvis or by winning a Chicago contest. He got there by marrying Viv.

Yes, I said *marrying.*

He called to tell me the news one night while I was doing my homework: algebraic equations. Fun. "I wanted you to be the first to know," he shouted into the phone with music blaring in the background. "I proposed to Viv at the show I was doing tonight. We're going to get married this summer."

This might have been a complete surprise to me except that Ivory had already hinted that something like this was going to happen. She had e-mailed me a few weeks earlier. "Check out your dad's horoscope. Romance rules his sign," she'd written mysteriously.

Romance and my parents was also something I didn't want to think about.

Dad and Viv got married in June at the Elvis Wedding Chapel in Las Vegas. Where else, right? Dad wanted me to be there for the ceremony, so I flew to Las Vegas with them. The chapel was inside a hotel, although the place was a lot smaller than I expected. More like an Elvis living room than a church. There were just six white-painted pews and a small keyboard at the front.

The master of ceremonies was an Elvis impersonator named Tony who seemed like a nice guy, even though he had major wig problems. Every time he'd lean over to read from his notes during the ceremony, his Elvis wig would inch forward. He'd read a line and have to push his wig back into place.

"We are gathered here today [push wig up] to celebrate the marriage of [push wig up], Jerry Denny and Vivian Mahoney [adjust gold sunglasses]."

It was pretty humorous.

But he could belt out Elvis's songs. The way he sang "Love Me Tender" at the end of the ceremony probably would have brought tears to most people's eyes. Not being a big fan of love songs in general, I stared at my shoes throughout the entire piece, hoping the musical torture would end soon. Even though there were only four of us and two wedding assistants in the room, everybody still clapped when he finished because you always clap for somebody being Elvis. "Outta respect for the King," my dad says.

Ivory and I sat in the first pew during the ceremony. She had dyed the front part of her hair pink, and when my mom saw the official Elvis Wedding Chapel photo I brought home, I think she was kind of shocked. (Okay, a lot shocked.) There we were: pink-haired Ivory, me with a zit starting on my chin, my dad in a Hawaiian shirt, Viv with some overly large white flower stuck in the side of her shiny penny-colored hair, and of course—in the back of it all—our smiling, wig-wearing Elvis named Tony.

Pointing at the picture, my mom said the pink-haired girl looked like she was going to be trouble someday. I told her Ivory was okay. "She isn't as strange as she looks," I said. Although, in fact, she was.

The wedding only took about thirty minutes, including the pictures—and yes, the vows really did include the words "I promise to be your hunk-a hunk-a burning love forever." My mom would never, in a *million* years, have gone for that. But Viv just looked over at my dad, laughed, and answered, "I do."

My stomach felt kind of strange throughout the whole ceremony. All shook up. That's what Elvis would say. I was going to be related to Ivory. To Viv. To Viv's Vintage. To more of Chicago. *Jeesh, too weird to think about.*

After the wedding, we decided to walk to a restaurant across the street—Chinese, my dad's usual choice—because it was way past lunchtime. As we headed out of the hotel, I asked Ivory how Digger was doing. "Paul," she said, correcting me. "He's going by his real name now. You wouldn't recognize him. He's lost about twenty pounds." She held up her wrist, which had a green leather band etched with flowers and ivy. "His latest creation."

"And how's Gladys?" I asked because I knew from my dad that she had been moved to a nursing home at the beginning of May. At the time, my dad and Viv were pretty upset about it, but there wasn't much they could do. She'd been having a lot more bad days than good ones.

Ivory said Gladys was doing okay. "She asks about you a lot."

"Me?"

Ivory mimicked Gladys's voice. "She says, 'When is Elvis's friend—that polite young man who sat next to me at the show—going to stop by and see me again?'" I promised myself I would visit Gladys when we got back from Las Vegas. Maybe I'd even smuggle in a box of donuts, too.

While we waited on our food at the Chinese restaurant, my dad told us he and Viv had a special announcement to make. Right away, my mind thought the worst, of course. *Please don't say you're planning to have an Elvis baby.*

But thankfully, the news turned out to be about Viv's Vintage, not babies. The store was going to be expanding, my dad said. He and Viv had decided to add a new area: a vintage shoe room called Blue Suede Shoes. "It's a corporate merger," my dad explained, smiling widely at Viv. "I'm going to help out in the store when I'm not busy being Elvis, and Viv will help out at my shows when business is slow. From now on, we'll be known as"—he gestured at an invisible sign in the air—"Viv's Vintage and Jerry's Blue Suede Shoes. Won't that be great?"

Note to anybody in Chicago: If you're looking for a nice pair of patent leather shoes or a plaid polyester suit, now you know where to go.

At the end of the meal, the waiter brought out some fortune cookies for us. Ivory and Viv got the same fortune, something like, "A positive attitude creates a positive day." Mine said, "Your smile fills a room," which might have been okay advice for Miss America but wasn't very helpful for a guy.

My dad opened his cookie last and started laughing when he read the fortune. "I can't believe it," he said. "It's from Elvis."

"What?" We leaned across the table, trying to see the paper.

"It's a line from the song 'Don't Be Cruel.' It says, 'The future looks bright ahead.'" My dad looked up and smiled at the three of us. "I gotta agree with the King," he said in his Elvis voice.

No matter what the future held, I was pretty sure of one thing—the King would be a big part of it. Because, trust me, Elvis is everywhere.

255

Thankyaverymuch.

A Little More About Elvis

Elvis Presley (1935–77) remains a legendary figure in the world of music. Say his name and almost everybody has a story. Born in Tupelo, Mississippi, Elvis Presley came from humble beginnings. His mother, Gladys, bought him his first guitar at the age of eleven. In 1953, he went to Sun Records to record two songs as a gift for her. Three years later, he cut "Heartbreak Hotel," which became his first gold record, followed by more hits like "Don't Be Cruel," "Hound Dog," and "Love Me Tender."

In addition to singing, Elvis appeared in thirty-one motion pictures from 1956 to 1969. His career was interrupted briefly when he was drafted into the army for two years, but he returned to popularity wearing black leather and singing to a small stage audience in his televised "comeback special" concert in 1968. The 1973 Hawaiian concert (where he wore the famous Aloha Eagle jumpsuit) was the first concert ever broadcast by satellite around the world. In his later years, he was a popular Las Vegas performer, often opening his concerts with the dramatic theme from *2001: A Space Odyssey*.

Although more than thirty years have passed since his death, Elvis Presley's music and legendary stage presence live on. Today, it's estimated that as many as thirty thousand people around the world perform as Elvis impersonators—or Elvis tribute artists (ETAs). While working on *All Shook Up*, I watched shows by both amateurs and professionals. I saw performances by Las Vegas Elvises, Canadian Elvises, Ohio Elvises, nationally known Elvises—and even an eight-year-old Elvis. (I managed to get a few of my own Elvis scarves, too.)

What I noticed about all of the tribute artists I met was their appreciation for Elvis's music and their love of performing. They consider it an honor to bring back memories of Elvis for people who grew up with his music—and for those, like me, who didn't. I believe they share the best side of the King: his music, his legendary performance style, and his generosity and kindness to his fans. Like Elvis, tribute artists sign autographs, give out scarves, shake hands, and raise money for charity at their shows.

Most tribute artists re-create Elvis's look by wearing authentic reproductions of his costumes and jumpsuits, which are known by names like the Gold Lamé, the Peacock, the Powder Blue, and—of course—the Aloha Eagle. Some professional tribute artists perform with a full band and backup singers, too. I heard Elvis's former drummer D. J. Fontana and backup singers the Sweet Inspirations perform at one special tribute concert. I've also talked to a lot of people who knew somebody—who knew somebody else—who once met Elvis. The *real* Elvis.

In a speech, Elvis once said, "I learned very early in life that without a song, the day would never end. Without a song, a man ain't got a friend." He recorded more than seven hundred songs in his lifetime. My all-time favorite? "Walk a Mile in My Shoes."

But don't look for me to be performing it onstage anytime soon.

Special Thanks

I'd like to offer my own "thankyaverymuch" to my editor, Joan Slattery, my husband, Mike, and my three student readers, Daniel Kuerbitz, Ellen Kuerbitz, and Nick Cirino. And a big *hunk-a hunk-a* hug to all of the Elvis tribute artists who answered my questions and shared their music with me. Special thanks to Ohio's own "Danny G" and Canadian tribute artists Mario Cervini and Kevin Bezaire.

Also by Shelley Pearsall
Trouble Don't Last

Eleven-year-old Samuel was born as Master Hackler's slave, and working the Kentucky farm is the only life he's ever known—until one dark night in 1859. With no warning, cranky old Harrison, a fellow slave, pulls Samuel from his bed. And, together, they run.

The journey north seems much more frightening than Master Hackler ever was, and Samuel is not sure what freedom means aside from running, hiding, and starving. But as they move from one refuge to the next on the Underground Railroad, Samuel uncovers the startling secret of his own past—and future.

"Powerful . . . a suspenseful, emotional story."—*USA Today*

★ "Action packed . . . gripping from beginning to end."
—*Publishers Weekly*, Starred

★ "Astonishing . . . a thrilling escape story."—*Booklist*, Starred

Winner of the Scott O'Dell Award for Historical Fiction
A *Booklist* Top 10 Historical Fiction for Youth Selection
A *Booklist* Top 10 First Novel for Youth
A Bank Street College of Education Best Children's Book of the Year
A Virginia Library Association Jefferson Cup Honor Book
Winner of the Ohioana Book Award

Also by Shelley Pearsall
Crooked River

The year is 1812. A white trapper is murdered. And a young Chippewa Indian stands accused.

Captured and shackled in leg irons and chains, Indian John awaits his trial in a settler's loft. All the while, thirteen-year-old Rebecca Carver sleeps and cooks and cleans below, terrified by the captive Indian right in her home.

In a world of crude frontier justice where evidence is often overlooked in favor of vengeance, Indian John struggles to make sense of the white man's court. His young lawyer faces the wrath of a settlement determined to see the Indian hang. And Rebecca must decide for herself what—and who—is right. At stake is a life.

From the award-winning author of *Trouble Don't Last* comes a fast-paced drama told in the alternating voices of Indian John and Rebecca Carver. *Crooked River* offers a probing look at prejudice, early American justice, and the true meaning of courage.

★ "A captivating tale of fear, ignorance, and bravery
on the Ohio frontier."—*School Library Journal,* Starred

★ "This vivid look into the reality of crude frontier life and justice is
outstanding historical fiction. . . . As Reb tries to sustain a life,
Pearsall brings a snapshot of history to life."
—*Kirkus Reviews,* Starred

A Great Lakes Book Award Nominee
An NCSS-CBC Notable Social Studies Trade Book for Young People
A New York Public Library Title for Reading and Sharing
A New York Public Library Book for the Teen Age